D0387058

TURTLEFACE AND BEYOND

TURTLEFACE
AND BEYOND

..

ARTHUR
BRADFORD

STORIES

FARRAR, STRAUS AND GIROUX   NEW YORK

Farrar, Straus and Giroux
18 West 18th Street, New York 10011

Grateful acknowledgment is made to the publications in which
these stories first appeared, in slightly different form:
Cousin Corinne's Reminder ("Resort Tik Tok"), *Five Dials* ("Travels with Paul"),
McSweeney's ("Snakebite"), Nerve.com ("Orderly" and "Wendy, Mort, and I"), *One Story*
("217-Pound Dog"), *StoryQuarterly* ("Build It Up, Knock It Down"), *Tin House* ("Turtleface" and "The LSD and the Baby"), and *Vice* ("Lost Limbs").

Library of Congress Cataloging-in-Publication Data
Bradford, Arthur.
    [Short stories. Selections]
    Turtleface and beyond : stories / Arthur Bradford. — First edition.
        pages   cm
    ISBN 978-0-374-27806-9 (hardback) — ISBN 978-0-374-71284-6 (ebook)
    I. Bradford, Arthur. Turtleface.   II. Title.

PS3602.R34 A6 2015
813'.6—dc23

                                                                      2014027441

Designed by Abby Kagan

Farrar, Straus and Giroux books may be purchased for educational, business,
or promotional use. For information on bulk purchases, please contact the Macmillan
Corporate and Premium Sales Department at 1-800-221-7945, extension 5442,
or write to specialmarkets@macmillan.com.

www.fsgbooks.com
www.twitter.com/fsgbooks • www.facebook.com/fsgbooks

1   3   5   7   9   10   8   6   4   2

To Maggie Vining

Oh! Why I want to see
every leaf on every tree.
Who put all this burden on me?

—HOLCOMBE WALLER, "ATLAS"

CONTENTS

We were paddling our canoes down a remote, slow-moving river, a full day's travel in either direction from the nearest road, when Otto decided to do something spectacular and stupid. Around a bend we encountered a sandy cliff rising up out of the water. Otto announced he would climb the cliff and then run down its steep face. We could all take pictures as he descended in long Olympian strides. At the end of his run, as he neared the base, Otto explained, he would launch himself into the river, a down-hill running dive. It was late in the afternoon and we had all been drinking beer and whiskey.

Otto and I paddled to the cliff's base and he got out. Then he climbed. It was tough going due to all that loose sand.

"How's this?" he shouted down. He was about halfway up.

"Higher!" I shouted back. I was excited about the stunt and reasoned that greater height would maximize the effect.

I was feeling envious as well. Sheila and Maria were in the other canoe, watching intently. They wore cutoff blue jeans shorts over their swimsuits. Sheila was a photographer. She pointed her large-lensed camera up at Otto. Maria, my girlfriend, was a nurse and on the verge of dumping me for a number of legitimate reasons. At that moment I wished I possessed Otto's imagination and daring.

There was one other person with us, a cousin of Sheila's, named Tom. He was a large fellow who had joined the trip at the last minute. He couldn't, or wouldn't, paddle because he had broken his thumb. Instead, he declared he would be in charge of doling out the beer, and he spent the day sprawled in the center of the women's canoe doing just that. His skin had turned from pale white to dark crimson over the course of our journey. Maria had warned him about the dangers of exposure to the sun but he dismissed her advice with a wave of his cast-bound hand.

"I'll be fine," said Tom.

Otto reached a point on the cliff where he could climb no higher. The terrain above him was too steep. He was perhaps a hundred feet above the river now, clinging to exposed tree roots for support. Clods of dirt tumbled down the slope and bounced into the water in front of us.

"Do it!" shouted Tom. He threw a half-full can of beer toward the cliff, where it landed without a sound in the sand.

"Are you going to pick that up?" asked Maria.

"Nope," said Tom.

"I'll pick it up," I said. I paddled my canoe back toward the cliff.

"Are you ready?" shouted Otto.

"Yes!" I shouted back.

"Where should I dive?" asked Otto.

I could see that Otto was having second thoughts. But the cliff shot straight into the river and the water below it was dark and deep. It all seemed fine to me.

"Go to my left!" I shouted back, pointing to a general area.

"My steps are going to be so long, man!" shouted Otto. "Watch this!"

Otto gave a halfhearted whoop and leaped into the air. He took one huge stride, and then another. He was right about those long steps. He covered a tremendous amount of ground with each leap, such was the pitch of the terrain. The sun shone down and sand kicked up behind him, creating an impressive, super-human image.

Sheila clicked away with her camera and said, "Oh wow." Maria nodded appreciatively.

Admiration and envy swelled within me. I should have come up with this, I thought, or at least climbed up there and done it with him, a tandem performance. We could have shared the glory. The women would have rubbed our backs around the campfire that night while recounting our heroics. Otto's body pitched forward as he neared the river's edge. He was losing control, legs scrambling, barely able to keep up with his downhill momentum.

"Ahhh!" he cried.

He dove forward, flying out toward the water, and hit the surface with a smack.

Ouch, I thought.

"Whoa, fuck!" said Tom, slapping his knee with his one good hand. "Damn!"

The women were silent, unsure whether to laugh or be concerned. I moved closer to where Otto had landed. His body floated up in an awkward manner, facedown, arms splayed out from his sides.

"Turn over, Otto," I said out loud.

Maria yelled at me, "Get him, Georgie!"

I swam out and flipped Otto's body over. His nose was smashed. Something was wrong with his lip too. Otto took a huge gasp of air. He was alive, a good sign. I recall thinking, *Oh, this isn't so bad.*

"He's okay!" I called to the others. "He's all right."

"No, he's not," said Sheila.

Blood began to spill from Otto's nose and mouth. Sheila was

right. I had been too optimistic. He wasn't okay at all. Where was this blood coming from? What was wrong with his face? It was punched in. Jesus, how did that happen? It was just water.

We hoisted Otto on board Sheila and Maria's canoe. Tom got out begrudgingly to make room in the center. He stood next to me in the river while Maria, the nurse, attended to Otto's face.

Sheila kept saying, "Oh Lord. Oh my Lord."

Tom opened a new beer and together we scanned the water where Otto had landed, looking for the rock or tree limb that must have caused the damage.

Eventually Tom said, "There's your culprit."

He pointed to a dim, submerged object spinning in the current just below the surface.

"What is it?" I asked.

We watched for a moment as the object rose up, wiggled a bit, and then sank down.

"It's a turtle," said Tom, almost chuckling. "He hit a fucking turtle."

"Oh God," I said.

It was a small snapping turtle, the size of your average pie. It was injured, too, and struggling to remain upright in the water.

I waded over and fished the creature out of the river. Its shell was cracked and I could see tender insides through the gap.

"Oh no," I said.

"Tough day for him," said Tom, shaking his head.

Over in the canoe, Otto coughed and moaned.

"What happened?" he sputtered. "What?"

"We need to get him out of here," said Maria. "We need a hospital. A helicopter, something."

Of course, there was no hospital or helicopter anywhere nearby. Our cell phones had lost any kind of signal long before we had even put the boats in the water that morning. I thought about shouting or blowing a whistle, but it really was no use. We'd simply have to paddle Otto downriver as fast as we could.

Our plan, before this happened, had been to camp out on a sandbar and reach the road crossing early the next day. From there one of us would hitchhike back up to the vehicle we'd left at the starting point. It was a plan hatched by a group of people in no particular hurry.

We fastened Otto down as well as we could. He was conscious, but dazed and in shock. The only lucky element in our situation was the presence of Maria, the nurse. She tended to him with improvised bandages and ice from the coolers. Even if there really wasn't much that could be done for Otto right then, we all felt better knowing that someone competent was involved.

Because Maria was occupied with her patient, that boat needed another paddler. I took her spot in the stern and Tom, broken thumb and all, was given the task of paddling the second boat solo.

"I can't do this," he protested.

"Jesus, Tom," said Sheila. "This is an emergency."

We shifted most of the gear into Tom's boat to make room for both Otto and Maria in the middle of ours. As we readied to leave, I made a spur-of-the-moment decision. I fished the injured turtle out of the river. Then I emptied one of our coolers and placed the turtle inside it, with a little bit of river water. I put the cooler in our boat, under my seat.

Tom watched this procedure with disdain. "What the hell are you doing that for?" he asked me.

"We can't just leave him here," I said.

"We sure can," said Tom.

"We need to go," said Maria.

Sheila and I set out at a frantic pace and nearly capsized the canoe right at the start. It would have been proverbial salt in the wound, dumping poor Otto into the water just then, but we managed to keep upright and soon hit our stride. It wasn't long before we had left Tom far behind, cursing and swirling about in the current. He was in for a long, rough trip, paddling one-handed all by himself, but we didn't have time to worry about that.

We paddled past lush pine forests and stunning rock outcroppings, hardly noticing the landscape in our haste. The wild surroundings had seemed pristine and magical that morning, but now it all took on a desolate air, especially as the sun dipped lower and cast long shadows in the canyons. I kept hoping we'd meet up with another group or pass some lonesome cabin equipped with a radio, but there was nothing. At one point we startled a moose.

"Moose," said Sheila as we cruised past it.

"Wha?" said Otto.

"Shh . . ." said Maria. She had been talking to him throughout our journey, gently waking him from time to time to be sure he didn't slip into a coma.

"How's he doing?" I asked.

"Stop asking me that," said Maria.

"How's the turtle?" asked Sheila.

"Not so good," I reported. I held the cooler steady between my feet. The turtle lay still, listlessly sloshing about in the water, retracted inside its cracked shell.

Night fell and still we hadn't reached the road. Maria pointed a flashlight ahead of us so that it cast an eerie beam across the water, and we forged on. My hands were blistered and my shoulders numb. Sheila could barely lift her arms. She puked over the side of the canoe and collapsed. I felt a wave of admiration for her then, paddling so hard her body gave out on her. She hardly knew Otto, by the way. They had only been dating for about a week before embarking on this trip. We pulled over and Maria gave

Sheila water and massaged her arms. Then they switched places. Maria placed a cool, wet bandanna over Otto's face.

"Don't lift it up," said Maria as she took the bow.

We made good time with Maria's fresh arms and reached the bridge crossing around midnight. This felt like progress, except we soon found that there were no cars traveling the road at that hour.

"Fuck," said Maria. "We should have paddled faster." This comment seemed directed at me, since Sheila had clearly done all she could.

We dragged the canoe onto the shore and left Otto inside it. Maria grabbed a cell phone and ran down the road looking for a signal. Sheila and I stayed behind with Otto, both of us too tired to run around the wilderness on such an errand. Otto kept at it with his raspy wheezing and intermittent coughing fits. Awful as he sounded, the noises offered a bit of comfort. When he was silent we worried that he might stop breathing altogether.

Sheila and I fell asleep in the dirt next to the canoe and woke up hours later to the sound of a truck engine. It was nearly dawn. A logging rig had picked up Maria several miles up the road. They'd managed to contact the state police and a trauma unit was on its way in a helicopter.

I woke Otto up and told him help was coming.

"Help?" he said. "What's the matter?"

"Do you remember what happened?" I asked him.

Otto was silent. I pulled the bandanna away from his face and let a bit of light from my flashlight shine upon him. Maria had done a good job cleaning things off, but now the swelling had set in. It was a gruesome sight, hardly recognizable as a face. Something had shifted, or disappeared. *Where is Otto's nose?* I thought.

Finally Otto said, "I'm in a canoe."

"Right, right," I replied.

"And you told me to run," he said.

"Well, no, you decided to run," I pointed out. "You were on a cliff."

"And you told me . . ."

"No, you had made up your mind . . ."

"Stop bothering him," said Maria.

"Okay," I said.

I got up and approached the loggers who had picked up Maria. They were standing beside their truck smoking cigarettes in the dim light.

"Our friend is hurt," I told them.

"We know that," they said.

"Do you have any tape?" I asked. "Strong, sturdy tape?"

"Duct tape?" said one of the loggers. "You want duct tape?"

"Right," I said. "Duct tape."

The logger reached inside his truck and pulled out a dirty silver roll.

"Like this?" he asked.

"Yes," I replied. "I'll give it back."

I took the roll of tape and found the cracked turtle in the cooler. I placed a strip of tape carefully over the break in its shell, as much to keep things out as to keep them in. The turtle's head and legs remained retracted and it was difficult to tell if it was even alive. Maria watched my efforts with disdain.

"When this is all over you and I need to have a talk," she said to me.

"Okay, sure, I know," I said.

The sunrise brought a fresh round of blackflies and we swatted them away until the helicopter finally arrived. It hovered over the dirt road spraying dust and rocks in every direction. Three men jumped out with a stretcher and suddenly the place was bustling with activity. With crack precision they loaded Otto into the chopper and it was decided that Sheila and Maria would go along. I stayed behind with the canoe to wait for Tom.

The helicopter lifted off and things grew quiet once again. The loggers turned to me.

"You mind if we depart now?" one of them asked. "We're late already."

It occurred to me then that I might hitch a ride to wherever they were going. But I'd said I'd wait for Tom and those loggers didn't seem eager for my company anyway. "Go ahead," I told them. I gave them back their roll of tape and they left.

It seemed as if Tom should have arrived by then. I decided he must have stopped somewhere when it got dark. He was probably sleeping in, hoping for the problem to get solved before he arrived on the scene. I washed the blood out of the canoe and settled in to wait.

I watched the turtle in the cooler. Toward noon his little nose poked out cautiously and my heart jumped. He was alive! I dipped his body into the cool river and cleaned him off as best I could.

Tom showed up that afternoon, wet and angry. His canoe was half full of water and all of the gear was gone.

"Where the hell is everybody?" he asked me.

"A helicopter came," I said. "They went to the hospital."

"A chopper? Here? Aw, fuck." Tom held up his hand. The cast over his thumb had mostly crumbled away.

"I think I'm going to need a doctor too," said Tom. "They should have waited for me."

"Otto was in bad shape," I pointed out.

"Yeah, but . . . look at this," said Tom. He motioned toward his swamped canoe. "I could have died back there. You assholes abandoned me."

Tom was drunk. Although our gear was gone, he had managed to save a few beers. He offered one to me.

"Thanks," I said. The beer tasted terrible and I felt immediately dizzy because I hadn't eaten anything since the day before.

Tom peered into my cooler, looking for booze, and saw the turtle, cleaned off and wrapped in tape.

"Well, look at this," he said. "You're a regular Doctor Doolittle."

"He's still alive," I told Tom.

"He's not going to survive."

"You might be right."

"Oh, I'm right. You know what we're going to have to do?"

"What?"

"Eat him."

"The turtle?"

"Right," said Tom. "It's the proper thing to do when you mortally wound an animal in the wild."

"I'm not going to eat that turtle," I said.

"Look," said Tom, "it's more respectful than letting him die in vain. That little fella was doing fine until you and Otto decided to fuck up his day. Now you just want to tape him up and flee the scene. Show some respect, Georgie. It's the least you can do."

"Hold on," I said. "What do you mean by 'you and Otto'? It was Otto's decision to run down that cliff. I was just there to provide support. We all were."

"I had nothing to do with it," said Tom. "I wash my hands of the matter. Except this turtle here. I'll help you make a soup if you want. I'm hungry as hell and the meat will go bad if we wait much longer. It's the law of the jungle, Georgie. Eat what you kill. Leave no trace."

I had no response for this logic except to say that we were not going to eat the turtle and the matter was no longer up for discussion. About an hour later we caught a ride to our car in the back of a pickup truck. I held the cooler with the turtle on my lap, trying not to let it bounce too much on the dirt roads. Tom clutched his broken thumb and moaned.

Back at home I took charge of the turtle's rehabilitation. I visited a veterinarian, who offered a grim prognosis.

"It won't survive," he said. "The wound is too severe and infection has set in. I don't know why it's still alive, to be honest."

Against his advice I paid $800 to have an antibiotic IV inserted into the turtle's small vein. I also learned that it was a female turtle, not a male, as I had for some reason assumed. I named her Charlotte, after an elderly woman I once knew who sort of resembled a turtle. I purchased a plastic children's wading pool and filled it with rocks, water, and moss-covered tree limbs. This I placed inside my small apartment to provide a habitat for Charlotte. If she was going to die, I reasoned, it would be in relative comfort.

Otto was laid up in the county hospital for nearly a month. They treated several infections, brain swelling, and did their best to reconstruct his face. The doctors and nurses there kept commenting on how lucky he was to be alive.

"I'm not lucky," Otto would tell them. "I ran into a turtle."

I visited Otto often during his recovery, a gesture meant to be kindhearted, but somehow interpreted as an effort to ease my own guilt.

"Ah, so you're the accomplice," remarked one of Otto's attendants upon my arrival.

"I wouldn't call it that," I said. "I was just there at the time."

"You told me where to dive," said Otto, sipping on a blended fruit shake.

"When I told you that, there was no turtle in the water."

"Well, how could you know?" said the attendant, smiling in an odd placating manner that I've come to believe is taught at medical institutions.

The swelling in Otto's face had subsided, but what was left now was an unsettling tableau not unlike one of those big rubber masks you sometimes see kids wearing on Halloween. His nose had been rebuilt into a small nub and remained shifted off to one side. He was missing a cheekbone, or something, below his left eye, so that side of his face was sunken significantly. He'd lost several teeth as well and now spoke out of the side of his mouth. It was an odd sensation, watching Otto heal up in the hospital. At times I felt jealous of all the attention and care he was receiving. He was the hero who had braved the cliffs and survived, albeit scarred. I was just the petty coward accomplice, the one who had watched from below and directed him toward the invisible turtle. I knew it made no sense to envy a man with injuries such as Otto's, but I did.

A wealthier, better-insured person would likely have had more options for reconstruction than Otto. As it was, he had no insurance at all, and once his condition was considered stable, he was given a mix of prescription pills and asked to leave. I was the only one there on the day of his release.

"Where's Sheila?" asked Otto.

"She's not here," I told him.

"Great. Fantastic."

As I mentioned before, Sheila and Otto's relationship had extended only a week prior to his accident, and throughout his stay at the hospital I could see her performing an awkward calculus in her head. How long must she stay with him? I guess she had determined his release date was as good a time as any to move on, and I couldn't truly blame her.

You will not be surprised to hear that Maria dumped me as well. She had come to visit me in my apartment and gazed disdainfully upon Charlotte resting in the pool I had set up for her.

"This is ridiculous," Maria told me.

"She's doing better than expected," I pointed out. "She's begun to eat the food I give her."

"Your best friend is in the hospital," said Maria, "because of this turtle."

"Otto is not my best friend," I pointed out.

"That's not the point," she said.

"And it wasn't Charlotte's fault," I continued. "If anything, she's the victim here."

"That's not the point either," said Maria.

I had thought Maria might be impressed with my rehabilitation of the wounded turtle and see that I was indeed capable of compassion and competence, but that was not the case. She pronounced the whole situation disappointing, and left.

Once the paperwork was complete, Otto and I departed the hospital and located an organic food shop, where I bought him a fruit smoothie. He sipped it and gazed at the hustle and commerce on the street outside. You could see people walk by and do subtle double takes when they saw Otto's face, startling as it was.

"I guess everything just moved along without me," he said.

It was true. In fact, Otto had been evicted from his home while he was laid up as well. Apparently he had fallen behind on the rent long ago and his crafty landlord seized upon his absence to move his belongings to the curb.

"Can I stay with you for a while?" asked Otto. "While I figure things out?"

I said yes, of course, though my place was small, and already made more cramped by the presence of Charlotte and her pool. I had meant to tell Otto about Charlotte before we arrived, but it was a hard subject to broach, and so he simply came upon her when he arrived.

"What the fuck is this?" he asked me.

"That's Charlotte," I said.

Otto moved closer and saw the ridgeline on Charlotte's shell where the crack once was. It was a vicious scar, but few would have guessed at the sorry state she had been in. Charlotte was quite recovered at this point and, seeing Otto and the turtle together, it occurred to me that despite her smaller size she had fared better in the collision. Although it was also true that she was now confined to a plastic wading pool as opposed to living free in the wild. I suppose a sound argument could be formulated for either conclusion, now that I think about it.

"Is this the turtle I think it is?" asked Otto.

"Yes, Otto," I said. "It is."

"You kept this thing?"

"She was going to die out there," I pointed out. "Tom wanted to eat her."

"Eat a turtle? Like in a soup? Is that what he wanted?"

"I don't know. Yes, I think he mentioned making a soup."

Otto reached into the tank and pulled Charlotte out. He held her high in the air as her stubby legs flailed about.

"Careful," I said, "she might bite you."

"I ought to chuck this reptile out the fucking window," he said.

"Please don't do that," I said.

I moved toward Otto and he held Charlotte away from me, his damaged face twitching in anger. We remained stuck in an uneasy standoff as the water filter bubbled gently in the pool beside us. Charlotte retreated into her shell, ready for yet another shock to her system at the hands of my friend Otto. But he didn't have the stomach for such cruelty in the end. He flipped Charlotte back into the pool, where she landed upside down, and I quickly righted her.

"It wasn't her fault," he admitted nobly.

Otto was not a good roommate. He snored loudly and was up at all hours, pacing about and muttering to himself. Whereas he had once been a great outdoorsman, he now preferred to stay inside most of the day. On the few occasions he did venture outside, people could not help staring at his odd features. I even caught myself staring at times, such was the severity of his injuries. Every so often someone would approach me privately and ask what had happened. The story was always met with such incredulity that I took to simplifying it greatly.

"A diving accident," I would say.

On the rare occasion that someone asked Otto directly, he would usually answer, "A hockey fight." This explanation was always accepted without question.

Sometimes I would return to the apartment to find Otto deep in conversation with Charlotte. He would whisper things to her, observations about the TV show he was watching or snide comments about my housekeeping habits. Otto's injuries required him to blend up most of his food and he expected me to maintain a steady supply of fruit and yogurt as well as clean up the mess he made preparing his shakes. As he drank down his meals he would often sit beside Charlotte and gloat.

"No, Charlotte," he would say. "You can't have any of this! Turtles can't eat citrus."

These conversations would go on at all hours, sometimes

becoming so heated that I feared for Charlotte's safety. But for the most part it was just companionship. Where Otto had once seen Charlotte as the agent of his destruction, he grew to view her more as a comrade in arms. No one else understood what they had been through. I sometimes felt that they were forming an alliance against me, despite all I had done for them. We rarely spoke of the accident, but when we did Otto would always be sure to centralize my role in encouraging him.

"We all know why you took Charlotte home and nursed her so carefully," Otto explained to me. "Because of what you'd done."

"She needed help," I said. "If anyone should feel guilty, it's you. You landed on her."

"Ha!" Otto said with a laugh. "I should feel guilty? Look at me. Do I look like I should be feeling guilty about anything?"

Throughout this period Otto ingested vast amounts of pain medication and I began to suspect that he was playing several doctors at once for prescriptions. Meanwhile, preposterous bills relating to his hospital stay showed up in the mail.

"One hundred and forty thousand dollars!" screamed Otto. "How do they expect me to pay that?"

One of the bills suggested Otto call a helpline to discuss his situation, which he refused to do. I decided to call the number myself one afternoon. It turned out this wasn't a financial helpline, as I had thought, but rather a connection to some kind of support group for people who had experienced traumatic injury. I signed Otto up for one of their meetings and told them I'd bring him there myself.

"Why would I want to attend some shit like that?" asked Otto, after I told him what I had done.

"It might be helpful," I said. "You stay in the house all day long. It isn't healthy."

"Healthy? What does that even mean, 'healthy'?"

Otto retreated to the corner near Charlotte's pool, as was his wont. He stared in at her and whispered something I could not understand.

The next day Otto fashioned a small leash for Charlotte and announced he was taking her outside for walk. At first this idea seemed ridiculous to me, but it turned out regular constitutionals of this sort are recommended for captive snapping turtles and the practice proved to be enjoyable for both Otto and Charlotte. Of course, the walks were anything but brisk, and the two of them together presented an odd spectacle, eliciting even more attention than Otto had when he'd ventured out on his own. But Otto clearly took comfort in Charlotte's companionship, and I was thankful for the time alone in the apartment. Around town, Otto became known as "Turtleface," a moniker I did my best to hide from him.

When the time came for the first support group meeting, Otto put on his coat agreeably, then casually picked up Charlotte and wrapped her in a thin blanket.

"She's coming with us," he said.

"Okay," I consented. It seemed a small price to pay for progress.

The meeting was held in a classroom at the local community college. Otto and I walked in late and scanned the room, a semicircle of wheelchair-bound amputees and various examples of disfigurement. One man had a leg swollen up the size of a barrel.

"Oh fuck," said Otto, "would you look at this?"

"You're one to talk," said the man with the swollen leg. "And what's that, a turtle?"

Otto covered up Charlotte with his coat, a protective gesture.

"It's my turtle," said Otto. He seemed to think the man wanted to take it from him.

"Actually, the turtle belongs to me," I pointed out. "I was the one who nursed it back to health."

"We share custody now," said Otto.

"Why don't you two sit down?" said a small woman named Nadine. She was the facilitator. We sat down and joined the semicircle.

Although they were in compromised physical shape, the people before us seemed to be a fairly well-adjusted bunch. They told stories and laughed at their wild misfortunes. One woman had been mauled by a chimpanzee at the zoo.

"It was my own fault, really," she said, showing us the scars on her neck, back, and shoulders. "Everyone knows how strong a chimp can be when it's angry."

Another man had a mental affliction that compelled him to dump scalding hot liquid on himself whenever he discovered it was within reach. The coffee machine was kept in another room on his account. His face was shiny from all the burns he had suffered, and much of his hair was gone.

Otto had no sympathy at all for this person. "Well, I can tell you how to solve this problem," he said. "From now on don't pour any more hot water on yourself, okay? Just stop doing it."

The burned man looked Otto up and down. "Suppose I told you to stop running into turtles," he replied. "Would that help?"

Otto pulled Charlotte out of his coat and handed her to me. "Hold her," he said. "I'm going to kick this guy's ass."

Nadine stood up and expertly talked Otto down. Apparently this sort of confrontation was not uncommon when someone new entered the group.

"You seem angry," she told Otto.

"Of course I'm angry," he said.

Afterward, I felt that the support group had done little for Otto, but the next day he told me he had experienced an epiphany overnight.

"I've come to the conclusion that we need to return Charlotte to the wild," he said.

I was resistant to this idea at first. I liked Charlotte and had imagined that when Otto finally left my home the two of us would lead a content existence together. Perhaps you are aware that snapping turtles have life spans nearly as long as humans' and as such make for good long-term companions.

But Otto laid out his plan and I couldn't deny the simple logic of it. We would return to the location of their misfortunes. Charlotte belonged back in her homeland now that she was well. And the journey would be cathartic for us all, he claimed.

Maria wanted nothing to do with such an endeavor, but we managed to persuade Tom and Sheila to join us for the trip. It was late fall, and chilly, by the time we got everything together and set off. Tom brought along a crossbow because he claimed it was bow-hunting season and he hoped to shoot an animal of some sort.

"I'd be more than happy to dress and cook it for everyone while we're camped along the river," he said.

"No, thanks," said Sheila. She was a vegetarian.

Tom refused to apologize for wanting to eat Charlotte back when she had been injured.

"It would have saved us a lot of trouble," he pointed out. "Though I do support returning her to her natural state since the resources have already been wasted bringing her back to life."

"She was never dead," I pointed out.

"Close enough," said Tom.

Otto was stoic throughout the journey down the river. He spoke softly to Charlotte, who rode in a large cooler beside him, and pointed out the sights along the shoreline.

Tom and I took to drinking whiskey from a tin flask, and by the time we reached the sandy cliffs where Otto had crashed months before, I was feeling sick. We had gotten a late start that morning and the days were shorter at that time of year, so it was nearly dark.

"We'll camp here," declared Otto, "and release Charlotte in the daytime. She might get disoriented if we let her go at night."

"I'm going hunting," said Tom. He donned a headlamp and smeared mud on his cheeks. "I'll go get us some dinner."

Tom stumbled off into the woods and that was the last I saw of him.

I helped Sheila set up the tents and then passed out inside one of them. Outside, I could hear Otto making a fire and chattering away with Charlotte. He was full of energy and kept calling out for Tom. At some point Sheila crawled inside my tent and said, "I'm cold. Can I sleep with you?"

I woke up in the morning, naked, holding on to Sheila, who was naked as well. My arms and head were freezing, having been exposed to the cold all night. Sheila shivered and huddled farther beneath our blankets. She felt wonderfully soft and warm and I tried to remember what we had done together.

Eventually I wandered out of the tent and found the fire still smoking. The other tent was empty and one of the canoes gone. On Charlotte's cooler I found a note. It said:

WENT LOOKING FOR TOM —OTTO

The sun rose and things got warmer. I made myself some coffee and began to feel awake and good. I splashed some of the cold river water on my face and looked around for signs of Otto and Tom. It was all trees and wilderness. Sheila and I seemed to be the only humans for miles.

Up above me loomed those tall sand cliffs. Sheila was still sleeping and I decided Charlotte had been left in that cooler long enough. It was my understanding that Otto wanted to make some kind of ceremony out of releasing Charlotte back into the wild, but I overruled him. I placed the cooler in the remaining canoe and paddled across the river to the cliffs and the spot where Charlotte and Otto had collided earlier that summer. It was difficult to determine the exact place, but when I'd gotten close enough I opened the cooler and dumped Charlotte in the river. She landed sideways and spun about, bewildered at her new surroundings. She paddled up to the surface and poked her hooked snout into the air. She stayed there for a moment, floating, that sealed-up scar still visible on her bumpy shell. I imagined the other turtles would wonder at it, and perhaps she'd tell them of the strange land she had visited and the weird behavior of her caretakers. Readjusted now, Charlotte sank down below the surface, swiftly paddling her sturdy legs, and disappeared into the murk and sway.

I turned my attention now to finding Tom and Otto. I thought I might climb the cliff to get a better vantage point. From there I could call out for them and see the lay of the land. I fastened the canoe to a nearby tree and began to climb up the sandy slope, just like I should have done earlier that summer when I had meekly watched Otto from below. Stopping several times to catch my breath, I eventually ascended even higher than Otto had, until my feet were scratched and sore and my chest heaved from the exertion. I stood there gazing down at the ribbon of river beneath me and tried to steady my breathing.

I called out, "Hey, Tom! Otto! Tom! Otto!"

But no one could hear me. The river down there was just a whisper. I pictured Otto standing near this spot, trying to discern the directions I had called out to him. It wasn't my fault. It had all been his decision, of course. I could see that plainly.

Far below me I saw Sheila emerge from the tent, stretch her

arms, and gaze about. She was stark-naked, a female beauty in the wild. I felt like a god, or a ghost, peering down upon her, unseen at this great height.

And I thought I might do something daring then, something a little spectacular, and unexpected. I launched myself forward. One, two, three, four, five . . . giant long jumps down the mountainside. I cleared thirty, forty feet per stride! I was a monster, a freak of nature, hurtling toward the water.

"Hey, Sheila!" I called out, glancing her way, trying not to land on my face as I careened down the cliffside.

She looked about her, startled.

"I'm over here!" I shouted. I was nearing the bottom now, carrying impossible speed. I leaped out, shooting into the water, sleek like a dolphin, waiting for the pain.

A crashing noise filled my ears and then coldness walloped me from all sides. Fuck, the water was so cold. A sharp, aching pain shot up my genitals and I struggled to the surface, gasping for air. The current carried me downriver and I kicked a rock hard with my foot. I sputtered to the shoreline and flopped myself into the canoe, wheezing, unable to fill my lungs with enough oxygen. My big toe had been cut open by the rock when I'd kicked it and now it started to hurt, and bleed. I'd cracked the toenail and my head ached as well.

I heard a voice, Sheila, calling out to me. "Georgie! Georgie! Are you all right?"

"I'm okay," I said, holding up my hand, waving it above the gunwale so that she could see it. "I'm all right."

A moment passed during which I imagined Sheila standing there, still naked on the shoreline, worrying about me. I wondered if she'd even seen my great feat, that perfect running dive into the cold water. Again, I raised my hand up, and again I said, "I'm all right. I'm fine."

"I'll make us breakfast," called out Sheila. "Vegetarian sausage and eggs."

"Thank you," I called back. "I'd like that."

I stayed down there, lying on the canoe floor, not wanting her to see me just yet. I lay back on the bottom of that canoe and I listened to the water flowing underneath me and I began to feel very good indeed.

COLD
FEET

arlier that year, before the winter set in, I moved into a large farmhouse outside the northern town of Burlington, Vermont. It was a community living arrangement and my housemates were hippies who didn't believe in using fossil fuels for heat. There was hardly any point in heating that place anyway. It was thin-walled and drafty, built long ago by someone who didn't take the climate into account. I believe it was only meant to be a summer residence. This was why the rent was so cheap. At any given time there were a dozen or so of us living there. In the summer our numbers swelled and people slept on the porch and unkempt lawn, but that winter our ranks dwindled, and those of us who stayed were always cold and unwilling to admit it.

We wandered through the hallways draped in blankets, watching our breath condense in the air. We burned the furniture when we ran low on wood for the woodstove. At night we piled clothing and rugs on top of our blankets in an effort to hold in the heat. Each morning, we remained huddled underneath our dusty piles of fabric until nearly noon, too afraid to get up and face the chilly air. We conducted conversations by yelling from room to room.

"Did anyone feed the cat?"

"Which cat?"

"The yellow one."

"We don't have a yellow cat."

"Yes, we do!"

"Who put wheat germ in the toilet?"

I was lazy, but not the laziest. I'd stumble into the kitchen and the fire in the woodstove would be out and all the dishes would be locked in a frozen puddle in the sink.

"What the fuck?" I'd yell.

"Be quiet," someone would say, from under their covers.

It was my feet that were the coldest. I don't know why I didn't invest in sensible socks that year, or at least a good pair of slippers. What were we doing out there in the hinterlands anyway? We should have been seizing the day somehow, making our mark, but instead we stayed frozen in our inertia, justifying the fact that we couldn't get out of bed with our back-to-nature rhetoric. We were protecting the earth! By doing nothing!

I had a friend named William, an older man whom I admired because he lived an even more stark existence than we did. He was a hermit. His home was a one-room shack out in the woods and he had no electricity or running water. He spent most of his time loading firewood into his woodstove and drying socks on a clothesline hung across his ceiling.

That winter, one of William's relatives, concerned about his advancing age, had given him an electric generator and a small black-and-white television set. The hippies in my home wouldn't allow televisions, so I liked to venture out to William's shack in order to watch basketball games at night. That was my main social activity.

The TV set was tiny and got spotty reception, but on clear nights we could pick up the Boston broadcast of the Celtics' games. Previously, William had listened to the games on his transistor radio, but ever since the arrival of the TV he noticed that the Celtics began to win more often. He kept a chart on his wall calendar on which he noted the correlation between certain variables in our viewing habits and the scores of the games. For instance, if I sat on the wooden chair by the door and held on to the wire hanger which served as the TV's antenna throughout the fourth quarter, the Celtics outscored their opponents by five or more points. Likewise, the volume had to be turned down for the second quarter or they would find themselves behind at halftime. Whenever things seemed to be going badly for our team, William would rearrange our positions.

"Hold your arm up higher," he would tell me. "Both arms now, spread your fingers!"

The general rule was: the better the TV's reception, the better the Celtics played. As that long winter progressed we both became certain that the outcome of their season depended entirely upon our mastery of the rituals surrounding the use of that television set.

There was an outhouse next to William's shack and using it was an unspeakably cold endeavor. The wind would whip up though the hole and bite you in the ass. William had been a heavy drinker in his youth and one winter he passed out while sitting in that outhouse. When he woke up the cheeks of his exposed rear end were black with frostbite and later at the hospital they had to remove the dead tissue, leaving two divots in his posterior. The term "freezing my ass off" rarely means what it actually claims, but old William was a person who could rightfully say that he had done such a thing.

One stormy night I showed up at William's place a little late and he was upset.

"You've thrown the whole thing off!" he told me. "I can't get any reception. We're already down by fifteen points, you son of a bitch."

"I'm sorry, William," I said.

I took my seat and held on to the wire-hanger antenna. The

picture on the TV flickered in and out. The sound crackled but made no sense.

"What are we watching?" I asked. "I can't see anything."

William stomped about in a rage. He had a short temper and low tolerance for the presence of other people. This was, perhaps, the reason he was a hermit. He put up with my being there mainly because of the perceived impact on the TV's picture quality. Finally William sat down on his stool and grabbed my hand. It was an emergency move, a connection of bodies that sometimes aided in the TV's reception. All we could see now were little shadows dancing about on the screen. The sound was scratchy and hard to decipher. We sat like this for ten minutes perhaps, my soft, lazy, hippie hand gripped in his rough hermit paw. Eventually the wind outside shifted and the picture and sound became more clear.

"What is this?" said William. "What are they saying?"

The announcers were speaking French. This wasn't a basketball game after all. We were watching a hockey game broadcast from Montreal.

"Well, fuck," said William.

We scrambled to find the right station but by the time we did the Celtics were hopelessly behind. William sighed and settled into his chair, resigned to defeat. I loaded more wood into his woodstove. This chore had become more difficult for him recently. He seemed always out of breath. The hermit life was catching up to him.

"Can I use your outhouse, William?" I asked. He had a rule about not using it during the games, but since this one appeared beyond repair I thought it would be okay.

"Take a flashlight," said William. "Look out for the porcupine."

"The porcupine?" I asked.

"Right," said William.

William explained that he had been battling a porcupine that winter. It liked to gnaw on the wood underneath his home and outhouse. He'd attempted to shoot it, but had missed several times, and now he was worried the creature was out for revenge.

"I caught him waiting for me under the outhouse a few days ago," said William. "He was plotting to slap me in the ass with his spiky tail when I sat down."

I told William I thought this was pretty unlikely, but I took the flashlight out there all the same.

When I returned, the game was over and William sat gazing at the staticky image in front of him. He announced that he wanted the TV gone from his residence.

"The currents are ruining my thinking. It's too much information," he told me.

"So turn it off," I said.

"I can't," he replied. "It's stuck."

I didn't understand what he meant by that and I tried to click off the knob myself. It really was stuck. It wouldn't turn. I found a set of pliers and accidentally snapped the knob right off.

"Well done," said William.

The TV sat there blaring at us.

"Let's unplug it," I suggested.

"I already did," said William.

It was true, the set was unplugged, and yet the pictures and sound were still coming out.

"Well, that's unusual," I pointed out.

"Just get it out of here," said William. "I'd like to go to sleep."

So I took the set back to the farmhouse. It sat next to me on the passenger seat of the car as I drove, still chattering away. I carried it inside the house where the hippies were all gathered around the woodstove. They looked up at me like I'd brought a rotting carcass into their home.

"It won't turn off," I explained.

I wandered upstairs, set the TV on a stool in front of my bed, and got under the covers. I watched the evening news and a wrestling match and a French Canadian movie about a female detective, or insurance agent, I couldn't tell which.

A woman named JoAnne came into my room and asked if she could watch the TV too. We huddled together under my heap of blankets, staring at the flickering TV in my otherwise dark room.

"Your feet are so cold," she told me.

"I know, I know," I said. "They've been like that all winter."

JoAnne got out of bed and returned with a big pot of steaming hot water. We both put our feet inside it and it felt very good. It was the warmest my feet had been in months, maybe years. She was a compelling woman, this JoAnne, with short-cropped hair and dark freckles on her cheeks. We hadn't spoken much since she'd moved into the house a few months before. I had a feeling she was with someone else, but I invited her to stay in my bed that night and when she did I was grateful for the company, and warmth.

In the morning when I woke up the TV was just a quiet, dim flicker. Then it died and went silent. The pot of water where we had warmed our feet now had a thin layer of ice on its surface. I slipped out of the bed, where JoAnne was still sleeping, and I jumped up and down to get blood flowing to my frozen toes. The TV toppled off the stool and hit the floor with a crash. A pile of silver batteries spilled out of a compartment in the back. JoAnne woke up then and smiled sleepily.

"It was the batteries," I told her. "That TV wasn't magic after all."

"I knew that," she said.

Roger, a hippie from England, walked into the room, wide-eyed and wrapped in a blanket.

"Did I hear a crashing sound in here? Is he trying to hurt you, JoAnne?"

I was naked and growing cold. "It was the TV set," I told him. "It fell on the floor."

"Nevertheless," said Roger, "I'm confused by this situation."

I had been correct in thinking JoAnne had arrived at the house with a partner. It was Roger. My claim of ignorance was unconvincing.

"Go back to bed, Roger," said JoAnne.

"I shall not," said Roger.

JoAnne rolled over and covered herself in the blankets, leaving Roger and I standing there together. I didn't like being naked in front of him and couldn't find my clothing. I decided the best course of action was to get back into bed. JoAnne recoiled at the coldness of my body, but didn't object otherwise. Roger stayed in the room huffing about for an unreasonably long period of time, but then he finally left.

We got out of bed at noon and I drove JoAnne into town to buy her an egg-and-sausage breakfast. On the way there we warmed our hands in front of the car vents, which blew hot air from the engine.

"Ah, this feels good," said JoAnne.

The vents underneath, the ones which were supposed warm our feet, were broken, or blocked somehow. JoAnne took off her boots and lifted her feet onto the dashboard so as to make them warm as well. I wished that I could do the same, but I was driving, and assuming such a position would have been unwise.

After breakfast, we smoked some marijuana with the college kids in town and then it started to get dark. Up there in Vermont, in the winter, it got dark before 4:00 p.m.

"We lost a whole day," said JoAnne.

I realized that the Celtics were playing another game that night and wondered if William wanted his TV back. Perhaps he'd made a rash decision the night before and now regretted it. JoAnne and I returned to the farmhouse and discovered all of our belongings strewn about the front yard in the snow. Roger had done that.

We gathered our clothing and books as best we could and placed them in the trunk of my car. The TV set was out there too, cold and wet, but otherwise undamaged.

"I wonder if it still works," I said.

"I'll bet you it does," said JoAnne. She examined it closely and managed to fix the knob I had broken the night before. She was very handy.

"William will be pleased about that," I said.

We drove to William's place, way out in the woods. I asked JoAnne to wait in the car while I knocked on his front door. I didn't want to surprise him by bringing a stranger into his house. He was shy around women as well.

When I knocked on the door there was no answer. I thought this was unusual since William didn't drive and was always home at night. I peeked in the door and found that the house was warm and lighted but William was nowhere in sight. I thought for a moment he had disappeared into the wilderness, in search of that wily porcupine perhaps, but then I realized he was simply relieving himself in the outhouse. I could see the glow from his flashlight between the holes which the porcupine had gnawed in the lower walls.

I had then what I thought was a very clever idea. I grabbed the stiff broom that William used to sweep the snow off his front porch and snuck behind the outhouse. I made a sign to JoAnne to keep waiting in the car. I was in a hurry because I didn't want William to finish before I made my move. My plan was to stick the whisk end of the broom up through one of those porcupine holes and give old William a spiky poke in the ass. I figured the straw ends of the broom would feel somewhat like a slap from the quilled tail of a porcupine. The problem was, once I got close

I saw that the holes in the outhouse walls were too small for the head of the broom. I considered sticking the narrow end of the handle up there but judged this to be too un-porcupine-like. I was in a hurry, so I made a snap decision to reach my hand up there in the hopes of jabbing William's buttocks with my outstretched fingers. Perhaps they would feel like quills?

I pushed my arm through and grasped about in the darkness until I found my mark. There it was, William's skinny, divoted ass. I'd meant to jab it with my fingertips, but the angle was wrong and the motion was more of a tickle than grab. My expectation had been that William would leap up and fly out the door in terror while I chuckled away and quickly informed him of my witty ruse. What happened instead was William sat still for a moment while I timidly gripped his bony posterior. Then he calmly rose up, and as I struggled to remove my arm from the hole where I'd wedged it, he unloaded both barrels of his shotgun into the outhouse toilet.

"Hey!" I yelled. "William! Hey!"

I was lucky, because William used an old-fashioned gun meant for hunting rabbits and squirrels, and, even in those close quarters, his aim was poor. But still, the result was my hand got riddled with shotgun pellets and at first felt numb, but then began to sting and bleed profusely.

William, fairly confused, stepped out of the outhouse just as JoAnne came dashing out of the car and, like a superhero, tackled him into the snow.

"Wait!" I yelled.

JoAnne deftly removed the gun from William's hands and smashed it against a tree.

"Who the hell are you?" cried William, staring up at the wild-eyed woman who had disarmed him.

There was a lot of sorting out to do, with much shouting and accusing bandied about, but eventually I was able to explain to both William and JoAnne how the matter lay.

"I was trying to play a joke," I said, clutching my wounded hand.

"A god-awful joke, at that," said William.

"When did you start bringing a gun into your outhouse?" I asked him.

"It's my right to do so," said William. "When did you start bringing feisty women to my home?"

"Her name is JoAnne," I said. "She's a friend of mine. She fixed your TV and we thought you might want it back."

"Well," said William, "the Celtics *are* playing tonight."

We gathered in his little shack and JoAnne dressed my hand, picking out the shotgun pellets with a set of rusty tweezers and pouring iodine into the bleeding holes. Every time I looked down at the bloody mess I felt dizzy and thought I might puke. William comforted me by saying that I could now legitimately claim to be in that select number who have survived being shot.

"Although the circumstances were less than honorable," he added.

We placed the TV in its rightful spot and to our surprise the Celtics came on like gangbusters. The disappointing loss from the night before was forgotten as they poured in one unlikely shot after another. The voyage outside the shack seemed to have improved the television's reception, and although William had not welcomed a woman into his home in nearly a decade he took a liking to JoAnne and proclaimed that her presence was influencing things in a positive manner.

"This gal here has boosted the frequency," he said. "Perhaps you might return for future contests, JoAnne."

Then, toward the end of the third quarter, William collapsed and fell onto the floor. A strange foamy spittle gathered at the edges of his mouth.

"Oh Jesus," said JoAnne.

He was having a stroke, though we didn't understand that at the time. I tried to lift him back into his seat, but he kept slumping down. When I spoke to him he gazed up at me uncomprehendingly.

"Do you know where you are right now?" I asked William.

"Of course I do," he eventually said. "I'm in the mines. Why is it so dark? Hit the lights, will you, Raymond?"

"The mines?" said JoAnne. "Who's Raymond?"

William had worked in the asbestos mines as a young man, back before the stuff was outlawed. It had left him with weak lungs. I didn't know who Raymond was.

We piled William into my car and drove him to the county hospital, where they explained to us that he'd had a stroke and what that meant.

"He's going to take a while to recover," said the doctor. "He can't be living out in that shack anymore."

While I was there I had the doctor look at my hand. He said JoAnne had done a fine job of cleaning it out and if I was diligent I'd avoid infection. I couldn't help but feel my prank had played some part in old William's stroke.

"It's possible," said the doctor, "though the conditions for his collapse were present in the body long before you started tickling his buttocks."

I called William's sister, who lived down in South Carolina. She suggested he might stay with their cousin, a dairy farmer, or perhaps move into a nursing home.

"I don't think William would like that," I told her.

"Well, he hasn't got much of a choice, has he?" she said. "That's what comes of living in a shack by yourself for so long. He should have found himself a wife."

William recovered slowly in the hospital. He remembered

nothing about shooting me in the hand, which I considered fortunate. My hand healed up just fine, which was fortunate as well.

JoAnne was the one who first suggested we move William into the farmhouse with us. The hippies held a meeting about it beforehand. This was a rule of the house. We had to have a meeting before a new roommate was permitted to take up residence. Seeing as it was winter and several folks had abandoned ship already, there was plenty of space, even for a bedridden hermit.

"I'm concerned about the sanitary aspects," volunteered Roger. He was still bitter about JoAnne's betrayal and opposed any idea of hers regardless of its merit.

"He's been living in harmony with nature for years," I pointed out. "We could all learn something from this man."

"What did he eat out there in his shack?" asked someone.

"Potatoes and rice," I said.

"What about vegetables?"

"I'm not sure about that."

"Well, that's why he had his stroke, then," said Roger. "Improper diet."

This debate went on for some time, but eventually the "yeas" won out over the "nays" and William was installed in a corner bedroom on the ground floor. There was an open fireplace in there which JoAnne took to keeping lit and stocked with wood that we transported from his shack. Now that William was gone from there, the porcupine began making his presence known, gnawing away great chunks of the porch and doorway.

"Why does he eat the wood?" asked JoAnne.

"It's the salt," I said. "And the fiber perhaps."

"There's plenty of wood in the forest," said JoAnne.

"Well, maybe William was right," I said. "It's revenge for the time he tried to shoot him. We shouldn't tell William about this."

"Okay," said JoAnne.

William didn't mind how cold the farmhouse was, or, surprisingly, the constant flow of people in and around his room. For a hermit, he was quite social, and he regaled anyone within earshot with stories of the old days in the mines and logging camps where he had spent his youth.

"You kids are lucky you don't have to work like we did back then. Do any of you even have jobs?"

William's biggest issue at first was the lack of a television set on which to watch the Celtics' games. The hippies had voted to ban its presence. But finally JoAnne made an impassioned plea on his behalf, and, just as the Celtics began their late-season playoff run, the little black-and-white TV was fired up once again.

JoAnne had to rig up a series of wire hangers which stretched out the window and onto the roof in order to bring in proper reception, and William was very strict about the placement of each body in the room. At first the hippies avoided the TV and its commercial trappings, but then they began to creep in, warming themselves around JoAnne's fire and submitting with amusement to William's strict edicts concerning where they might sit and what positions were acceptable to assume.

"Since when did we take up watching sports in this household?" asked Roger.

"It's a communal activity," said a girl named Feather. "It gives us purpose."

I suppose this was true, and, in fact, I would say the same about William's general presence there. It gave us all a bit of a purpose. We fed and bathed him in his weakened state, and patted his back when the coughing fits struck hard. In return, he made us feel less useless and disconnected from the world "out there," the one we claimed to want to shun.

That was the year the Celtics made it to the NBA finals and beat the dreaded Los Angeles Lakers in six games, behind the storied

"Big Three" of Paul Pierce, Kevin Garnett, and Ray Allen. Those three got all the credit, but there was a houseful of us in northern Vermont who knew the truth behind that championship. We watched every game of that playoff run, moving accordingly in front of the magic television set, holding hands when we had to, in an attempt to make the picture more clear and therefore assist our team.

By the time the Celtics won the championship, the winter had finally faded. It was mud season then and the air was full of blackflies. William didn't last long once the warm weather set in. His lungs began to give out for good.

I tried to take him back out to the shack with me one day in early June but my car got stuck in the mud on the way there and he said, "Aw, to hell with it. I bequeath my belongings to the porcupine."

It was JoAnne who held William's hand as he took his last breath, lying there in that dusty bed at the farmhouse, and all of us sang some silly song before the ambulance arrived and took him away.

JoAnne left town that fall, after William had been buried. She headed for Alaska, where last I heard she was working on a fishing boat. I left the farmhouse as well, done, like so many hippies before me, with that particular experiment. On my way out of town I took a detour out to William's shack. Already the summer vegetation had grown thick around it. Already that little shack was getting swallowed up by the land. The door had been gnawed thin by the porcupine and inside there were little brown pellets, animal droppings scattered about the floor. I left the black-and-white TV set there on William's sunken armchair, plugged into the rusty generator with its wire antenna pointed skyward. It would be there for the porcupine, should he ever find the need to conjure its powers.

LOST
LIMBS

It wasn't until my second date with Lenore that I discovered one of her arms was missing. Our first meeting had been a blind date, arranged by a friend who had neglected to mention this arm situation. I suppose I'm not a particularly observant person. This is something I've been told on a number of occasions. Lenore wore a very well made prosthesis though, and I believe it was an understandable oversight on my part.

My next-door neighbor at the time was a magician named Clifford and on the weekends he performed at a club called Singing Henry's. There was no singer named Henry involved with the place. That's just what they called it. I decided to ask Lenore if she wanted to go see Clifford's magic show for our second date.

Lenore said yes and when I stopped by to pick her up I noticed there was a set of metal hook-pincers where her hand was supposed to be.

"Hey, what's this?" I said. I thought perhaps she was playing some kind of odd prank.

"It's my hand," she said.

"No, it's not."

"It's a prosthesis," she said.

She rolled up her sleeve to just below her shoulder so that I could see where her flesh ended and the device began. It was held on by a suction cup and two spandex straps.

"Well, okay," I said. How could I have missed that?

"Did you have that thing on before?" I asked. "When we went out before?"

"It's called a prosthesis," said Lenore. "I was wearing a different arm that night. It had rubber fingers. It's less noticeable, but not as useful."

Lenore stepped back into her apartment and retrieved the rubber arm. I still don't know how this device escaped my notice. Upon even a cursory glance it was immediately apparent that the arm wasn't real. The fingers didn't even move! But that's the way things are in life, I've found. Once you learn some fact, then all the clues become obvious and you feel like you should have known it all along.

The magic show was extremely lousy and I kept looking over to see how Lenore managed to clap with her prosthetic arm. She would raise it up a bit and then just pat down on the forearm part. This method didn't produce much noise, but Clifford didn't deserve much. Watching Lenore clap was more interesting than most of the magic tricks.

After each trick Clifford would yell, "And voilà!" and we'd all have to cheer for him. This became tiresome, but he did do one trick toward the end which I found impressive. He grabbed a live dove out of a cage, then he smacked it on its back really hard and confetti went flying everywhere. I got the impression the bird was supposed to disappear but instead it just stayed in his hand, looking stunned. So Clifford smacked it again, a little harder. This time the dove let out a little *squawk!* and more confetti flew into the air, but still it didn't fly away or disappear. I was beginning to feel bad for the bird and you could tell something was wrong because Clifford shook his head and pressed his lips to-gether. Then he just sighed and stuffed the dove into his pocket. His coat pocket! The show went on and I kept waiting for the dove to fly out or at least struggle in there, but it didn't move. Where did it go? It was amazing!

Afterward I asked Lenore about this and she said, "It just stayed in his pocket."

"A dove in his pocket?"

"Look, I don't know, maybe he killed it."

"What?"

"I'm kidding. I bet he tossed it away when we weren't looking."

I mulled this over but I'm pretty sure Clifford never tossed a bird offstage that night.

I asked Lenore if she wanted to come back to my place and she said, "No, thanks."

"Maybe we could just drive around a little?" I suggested.

"Why would we do that?"

"I don't know. It's easier to talk that way, when you are moving."

"You can just drive me home," said Lenore. "We can talk on the way home."

Once we'd started driving I said, "Well, Lenore, how did you end up losing that arm?"

"I was in a car accident," she said. "Actually, it was a van ac-cident. I was eleven years old. We were on a school trip."

"Did anybody die?"

"No."

"That's good."

"Yes."

"Did they try to sew your arm back on?"

"It was crushed. The van rolled over onto it."

"Oh. Well, I'm sorry."

"Sorry for what?"

"I'm sorry I didn't notice it before."

"I thought you did but you were trying not to mention it."

"Why wouldn't I mention it?"

"Most people pretend they don't notice it."

"I wouldn't pretend something like that."

"It's okay if you did."

"But I didn't."

I tried to kiss Lenore good night. She was a very attractive woman. She had these unusual irises that were light gray but had dark edges around them. She wasn't too interested in kissing me though. I thought about telling her how wonderful her eyes were, but this seemed like something she might have been told before. Another question occurred to me.

"Are your eyes real?" I asked her.

"What do you mean?"

"Are you wearing those colored lenses or something?"

"No, I'm not."

"Okay. I was just curious."

"Sure."

Our date ended on that uncomfortable accusatory note and I didn't see Lenore again for quite some time. Occasionally I would have these little fantasies, daydreams involving Lenore and her metal pincer hand. She'd stare at me with those light eyes while we made love and that other, rubber hand would lie on a table next to us, feeling left out of the action.

After the winter holidays my neighbor Clifford and I took a job with the city hauling away discarded Christmas trees and feeding them into a large wood chipper. Clifford's magic show didn't cover his bills, so he often took these temporary jobs to make up the difference. I did the same thing except I had no magic act to fall back upon.

On my second day at that Christmas tree job, a thick tree became wedged in the chipper's intake chute and I made the mistake of pressing my foot against the stump in order to force it through. My pants leg got caught in the in-feed rollers and pulled me into the machine. Luckily Clifford was right there and he yanked back the control bar, stopping the chipper and preventing it from sucking me all the way through. People get killed that way all the time! When I tried to remove myself from the chute though, it seemed that my leg was stuck.

Clifford kept saying, "You're going to be all right. I stopped the chipper."

"Then get me out," I said.

"I can't do that," he said.

"Why not?"

Clifford just said, "Don't look down there, okay?"

I wish I could tell you more accurately what it felt like to be lying there with my leg stuck in the chipper. I believe we all have this mechanism in our bodies which shuts off overwhelming pain. What's the point of registering such discomfort? All I felt was this very strange pressure telling me something was not right.

"Well, shit," I said to myself. "Who would've guessed my day would be turning out like this? Not me!"

And then I thought about Lenore. Perhaps this was how she had felt while that van was lying on her arm. I should give her a call, I thought. It had been over a year since our last encounter and as I mentioned before she'd been on my mind quite a few times.

An ambulance arrived at this point and they injected me with some chemicals which caused me to pass out.

● ● ●

I lost the lower part of my leg, almost to the knee. Chopped into mulch by that chipper! I learned this in the hospital once I woke up. To be honest, I was not overly alarmed at the time and thought it wouldn't be a great hardship living without this section of my leg, but it turned out I was wrong about that.

It took me months to get used to the prosthesis. On several occasions I stepped out of bed thinking I still had two feet and fell over onto the floor. I had those phantom pains too, where I thought my foot was itching or cramping up, but then I'd remember it wasn't even there! The city paid for my rehabilitation and eventually I made it back home and found an acceptable routine. It was then that I called up Lenore.

"I'm surprised to hear from you," she said.

"I'm surprised to hear from you too," I replied.

"You called me."

"Right, I know that. Listen, how would you like to go out on a date with me?"

"A date? Okay, I guess. How about lunch?"

"Great."

I picked Lenore up at her place, the same place where she had been living before, and we went for a drive out to the countryside. I'd decided we would have a picnic lunch, somewhere wide-open and beautiful. It would be a stark contrast with Clifford's half-assed magic show.

As we were driving I said to her, "I lost part of my leg."

"Your leg?"

"Yes, my right leg. I got caught in a wood chipper. That's why I'm driving with my left foot now, see?"

Lenore looked down. I'd learned to drive with my left foot. It was safer that way.

Lenore looked back up at the road and said, "There's a cat."

A cat jumped out in front of the car and I hit it.

"Oh man," I said.

I stopped the car and we got out. The cat lay in a heap on the road.

"Shit," I said. "Fuck."

"I think it's dead," said Lenore.

"I know it's dead," I said.

I took a blanket from my car, the blanket I'd been intending to use for our picnic, and scooped the body up as best I could. I placed it in the trunk. I didn't want anyone else to run over it.

There was a house nearby and Lenore said, "I guess that's where he lives."

"He or she," I corrected her.

"I bet it's a male cat," said Lenore. "Only male cats do things like that."

Together Lenore and I walked up to the house so that we could give the owner some bad news.

"You walk pretty well with that fake foot," said Lenore.

"I'm getting better at it," I said.

The house had a tidy appearance with an American flag flapping in the wind atop a metal pole. When I knocked on the door we heard noises from inside, but no one came out to see us.

"Maybe we can just leave a note?" I suggested.

"No, no. We can't do that," said Lenore.

It sounded like someone was moving furniture around in there.

"No one's answering," I said.

"Hello?" said Lenore.

The door flew open and a wiry bald man appeared before us. He was holding a shotgun at his waist. He pointed it first at me and then at Lenore.

"What's the problem here?" he asked.

"I believe we hit your cat," I told him, pointing at my car back on the road.

"My cat?"

"Right. It ran out in front of me. I'm sorry about this. Can you put down the gun?"

"Is that your car?" he asked me.

"Yes, it is. The cat ran right in front of me," I repeated.

"He's missing his leg," said Lenore. "He just lost his leg and couldn't stop in time."

This didn't seem relevant, or a particularly good excuse, but I suppose Lenore was trying to be helpful.

"Let's take a look," said the man.

I thought he meant to take a look at my leg, so I bent down to roll up my pants, but the wiry man poked me with the tip of his gun.

"What're you doing?"

"Showing you my leg."

"The cat," said the man. "Let's see the cat."

We walked back to the car, the man still pointing his shotgun at us.

"Do you think you could put that away?" I asked him again.

"No, I don't," said the man.

I opened up the trunk and uncovered the dead cat.

"Jesus fuck," said the man.

"I'm sorry," I said, again.

"You sure are. Where are the keys to this rig?" he asked me.

"The car keys?"

"Yes."

"Right here." I held them up.

The man snatched the keys out of my hand and said, "I'm taking these."

"Hold on," I said. I stepped forward and with surprising swiftness the old man swung the butt end of his shotgun around and struck my leg, the new leg, right where the joint ended. The prosthesis snapped loose and I fell over. I still hadn't gotten the fittings right. It was embarrassing.

"Hey!" said Lenore. The man pointed his gun at her and Lenore put her hands up in the air.

"It's just a cat," she said to him.

That's when the man noticed that Lenore had an artificial limb as well. She was wearing her rubber hand, the less practical of her artificial limbs, but of course harder to distinguish. "Aren't you two a fine pair?" said the man.

"Listen," I said, "I already told you I'm sorry about your cat."

The man walked up and yanked off my prosthetic leg. He tucked it under his arm and then said to Lenore, "I want yours too."

"Oh, come on," I said.

Lenore removed her arm and handed it to the man. He got into my car and drove away with both of our limbs, the picnic lunch I'd prepared, and that dead cat as well.

Lenore helped me up and I hopped over to a tree so that I could lean against it.

"That old shitfuck," said Lenore.

"At least we know where he lives," I pointed out.

"He better come back here," said Lenore. She was really mad. With her remaining arm she picked up a rock and threw it down the road in the direction he had gone. Her empty sleeve, the one which had covered up the artificial arm, waved about in the breeze.

We waited around for nearly an hour. I found a sturdy stick and used it as a crutch to assist with my walking. Lenore and I examined the man's house and thought about breaking in but a large dog lay asleep in the living room. He seemed friendly enough, but we opted not to take our chances there.

Instead we made our way down the road, me hopping with my arm draped over Lenore's shoulder for support. After a short distance we arrived at another house, this one less well kept than the old man's. Lenore knocked on the door and a hefty woman in a smock answered.

"We got robbed," said Lenore.

"Out there?" said the woman.

"We hit a cat," I explained, "and the owner stole my vehicle."

The woman let us inside, shaking her head. Her house smelled of cat urine and there were felines running everywhere.

"That was Henry who took your car," she told me. "Me and him don't interact much."

It was like a zoo in there! Cats pranced about on every surface, the shelves, the countertops, the stove. There were plates of stale food sitting on the floor.

"I don't suppose it was one of your cats I hit?" I asked her.

"It wasn't Henry's," said the woman. "He has a dog."

"Some people with dogs have cats," Lenore pointed out.

"Henry doesn't have any cats," said the woman.

"It was a black cat," said Lenore, "with some white spots."

"That was Elliot," said the woman. "He's deaf."

"Then I'm afraid he's dead as well," I said, "if that was him."

"I told you it was a male cat," said Lenore. She had been right!

The woman let us use her phone and I offered her $25 for the cat. I hoped she wouldn't take it, but she did. It was all the money I had.

The police arrived and the woman made us talk to them out front so that they wouldn't see all her animals. There was likely an ordinance against such hoarding. The police were unimpressed by the entire incident, including our lost limbs, but they gave us a ride back into town.

Lenore invited me to her apartment and we ended up having sex on her couch. It wasn't as enjoyable as I had previously imagined it might be. Perhaps we were both tired. It was a wool couch as well, so the fibers scratched our skin and made things itchy.

Afterward Lenore said, "I have a husband, so I'm afraid you'll have to leave now."

"A husband?" I said. "Where is he?"

"He'll be here in a few hours. He works late. He's a professional bouncer, so you really should leave."

"When did you get married?" I asked her.

"A while ago," she told me. It was a vague answer but I didn't feel like pressing the issue.

I called a taxi and as we were waiting Lenore told me something else. "I was born without my arm," she said. "I know I told you it was a car accident, but actually I was born this way."

"You told me it was a van accident. You said a van rolled over on it, not a car."

"Well, either way, it's not how it happened."

The taxi arrived and Lenore helped me down the stairs. They'd given me a crutch back at the police station but it was the wrong size and those stairs were pretty tricky.

About a week later a police officer showed up at my house with a package for me. It was Lenore's arm.

"This isn't mine," I told him.

The officer looked down at his notepad. "It says here you lost a prosthesis."

"I lost a leg prosthesis," I said. "This one belongs to my friend."

The officer looked down at my leg. I'd gotten a replacement by then. It was an ill-fitted temporary thing.

"Well, I don't understand this, then," he said, holding up Lenore's arm.

I convinced the officer to leave the arm with me and I made arrangements to bring it over to Lenore myself. When I arrived she was sitting on the wool couch with my leg attached to her arm. She waved it at me and smiled. A funny joke! We exchanged limbs and I tried to kiss her again but she wasn't having any of that.

"I'm moving to South America," she told me. "I'm going to work in an orphanage there."

"What about your husband, the bouncer?" I asked.

"He's gone. I'm not married."

"Oh," I said.

Her South America plan impressed me and I asked if I could join her, permanently. It sounded like a good, wholesome life. Lenore said it would be best if I thought things through before making such a move.

"That's a big decision," she told me.

And she was right! I had no business in Ecuador, or whatever country to which she was moving. Visiting Lenore was an option though, she made that clear, and lately I've been thinking I might take a trip down there to see just what's going on.

ORDERLY

It was an irresponsible thing to do. I even knew it at the time, but still I went ahead. I was working as an orderly at a facility called Riverwood Retreat, which wasn't really a retreat. It was a mental institution and a place for people with mild disabilities who couldn't function well in the outside world. Originally my job was to clean the residential areas, mop floors, disinfect bathrooms, and so on. But they were short on staff and after a few months I began to assist the professionals with the care of the residents. I would help lift someone from his wheelchair to the bed, or walk with a resident to the cafeteria and help him choose his food. I enjoyed these tasks more than the cleaning.

One of the residents was a strikingly pretty woman named Elsa. I couldn't figure out why she was there. She seemed to be in control of herself most of the time, though she did walk with a limp. She had a shock of gray hair running from the top of her forehead and very intense piercing eyes. Several times when I was in the cafeteria I noticed that she was looking at me. Her face had these sharp features and at first I thought she was angry with me about something. But then I began to understand that it was a look she always wore. Some people are just like that. They look angry even when they are feeling calm, or merely curious. I wondered if this was part of the reason Elsa had found herself residing here in the first place. One time I took Joseph, the resident whom I was accompanying, over to her table and we sat down next to her. Joseph had a visual disability and would feel all of his food with his fingers before he ate it.

"I hope you wash his hands before he does that," said Elsa.

I said, "We always wash up before we eat, right, Joe?"

"That's right," agreed Joseph, though now that I thought of it we had neglected to do so on that day. Elsa regarded his dirty fingers with disdain.

"My name is Georgie," I told her.

"I'm Elsa," she said.

I was going to extend my hand for her to shake, but I hadn't washed my hands either, and I figured she could tell. We ate the rest of the meal in silence.

Joseph told me that Elsa was "mental," that she would fly off the handle sometimes and then she would have to be restrained.

"They give her drugs now," he said, "and she's more calm."

I hadn't had much experience with women up until that point. In school, my advances had been met mostly with amused dismissal and it wasn't until later, when I fell in with the bass player of a local band, that I had what could be described as a relationship with a woman. That bass player was ten years my senior and left me for another woman, a turn of events which I took hard. I realized then that I had developed an attraction to older women. Elsa was perhaps thirty-five years old, and I found myself thinking about her quite a lot.

I suppose she could sense my interest. One time when I was eating with Joseph she walked by and brushed her hand across my back. I was very startled by this. I followed her out of the cafeteria and she handed me a folded-up paper towel and then turned away.

On the square of paper towel she had written, in crayon, "I am not crazy. Meet me. OK?"

By the time I had read it she was gone. I tried to figure out where she wanted to meet me and was frustrated at the vagueness of this request. But then, that afternoon, as I walked away from the main building toward the bus stop to go home, I saw her sitting on the side steps smoking a cigarette. Most of the residents were not allowed to smoke. She had permission though.

I walked up to her. "I read your note," I said.

"Good," she said.

"What did it mean though?"

"I can't discuss that right now," she said, looking away.

"Okay," I said.

We talked a while longer about things unrelated to the note. She told me she was from Wisconsin. She fidgeted a lot. Abruptly, in the middle of a sentence, she stood up and limped back up the stairs and went inside.

Like I said before, I knew it was irresponsible to be flirting like that with a resident. But she didn't seem "mental" to me. She just seemed nervous. And she was older than me. At that point in my life I assumed that wisdom came with age.

A few days later I was working an overnight shift and she startled me. It was nearly 4:00 a.m. and I was on the covered walkway between the residential halls. She darted out from the shadows and took hold of my arm.

"This way," she said.

We went into the exercise center and there she removed my clothes and then she took off her pants. I wanted her to take off her shirt too, but she wouldn't. She lay me down and climbed on top and we had very quick, hurried sex on one of the firm vinyl-covered mats. When it was over she grabbed her pants and shuffled off, leaving me there naked. I gathered up my clothes and finished my shift.

From that point on, whenever I had a night shift, we would meet up in the exercise room and have awkward, half-clothed sex. We rarely spoke and when my shift was over I would walk home in the dim morning light wondering if it hadn't been a dream.

This pattern continued for perhaps two months and then she stopped meeting me. I tried to catch her eye in the cafeteria during the day but she wouldn't even look my way. I was sad and a little heartbroken, but took it in stride. I was beginning to notice a pattern in my relationships with older women, or so I thought.

Elsa and I hadn't spoken or made eye contact in over a month when she approached me in the hallway and shoved another folded-up paper towel into my hand. This time she stayed there and waited for me to read it.

It said "pregnancy test."

"You took one?" I asked her.

She shook her head. "I need you to buy one," she said. "Buy one for me."

"You're pregnant?"

"I need you to buy a test," she said, "from a drugstore."

"Okay . . ." I said.

I fretted over this for hours until my workday was done. Then I went to the pharmacy and picked out the simplest-looking test. I was mortified to be seen buying such an item. I looked over the directions and it explained that the woman had to pee onto a strip of paper. The paper would show one red line if she wasn't pregnant and two if she was. What was it about pee that told you a woman was pregnant? I considered tampering with the test, peeing on the strip of paper myself so that the result would come out negative, but then I realized this wouldn't actually change things. I wasn't thinking rationally.

I returned to Riverwood and slipped the testing kit to Elsa. She thanked me and went on her way. I wanted to wait around for the result, but there was no good excuse for me being there after the end of my shift. So I went home and didn't sleep at all.

The next day Elsa handed me the little plastic tube which held the all-powerful strip. I took it from her, trying to gauge the results by the look on her face. I couldn't tell what was going on behind those pale eyes, though. I realized then, as I looked at her for an answer, that she really was crazy. By that I mean she wasn't living in the same world as the rest of us. Something about her gaze suggested an irrational state of mind. And then, a minute later, I stood alone in an empty closet looking down at the strip of paper she had peed upon, and I saw the two red lines declaring she was pregnant with a child we had made together.

I was terrified. I ran out of the closet and searched the hallways for Elsa. That crazy woman! We were going to have a crazy child! A nutcase baby! She was gone though, and people were staring at me running around like that. I left work early, without telling anyone, and I considered never going back.

I returned to the hospital a few nights later though, and I had a talk with Elsa. She sat on the cement steps looking up at me with her wide, shaky eyes, smoking one cigarette after another.

"I don't think you should smoke now," I told her.

"It calms my nerves," she said.

"It's bad for the baby."

"Babies don't smoke," she said, as if that somehow refuted the facts.

I asked her if she would consider having an abortion.

"No. Never," she said.

I felt the blood rush from my head and had to sit down. I sat next to Elsa and put my head between my knees. I know they say it is a miracle, the act of creating life. I know they say it changes you forever, for the better, when you see your first child born into the world. But I felt only fear that night, fear and some kind of awful wrath unleashed upon me for the things I had done. I began to cry and Elsa rubbed my back with the heel of her hand. She hummed a song too, a strange song I'd never heard, and it made no sense at all.

I wondered when the doctors would know about this. I wondered when I would get fired and if what I'd done was against the law and if so would I be put in jail. Over the next few weeks, as I watched Elsa walk around, I was sure I could see her belly growing. Other people must be noticing, I thought. I moped along thinking, *When, finally, is the shit going to hit the fan?*

I had a strange moment though, when I was back in that drugstore. I walked by the shelf where I had picked up that little pregnancy test and I stared at all the different-colored boxes thinking how each one was a box full of fate. Next to the boxes was a row of plastic bottles and some of them were labeled "Prenatal Vitamins." I grabbed one of those, stuffed it in my pocket, and left without paying.

I gave the bottle to Elsa and told her to take one a day, like the directions said.

"More pills . . ." she said to me.

"Take them," I said. "And stop smoking."

It would be an exaggeration to say that I loved Elsa, a huge exaggeration, but I did feel affection for her. And on this day I felt responsibility too. It was a new feeling.

It was during the night shift, a few days later, that I heard Elsa calling out my name. She wasn't yelling, she was just repeating my name steadily and it echoed down the hallway.

I ran to her room and saw that it was empty. She was in the bathroom down the hall. I tapped my fingers on the door.

"It's me," I said.

"Go away," she said.

I stood outside the door for two hours. Other staff members came and looked at me and one of the nurses called security. I wasn't supposed to be in the women's wing at that hour. I wasn't supposed to be standing outside the bathroom door like that, blocking the way, and not listening to anything anyone said.

The security crew arrived and I stood my ground. They hauled me away and as they did Elsa came out of the bathroom, finally. Her face was white and drawn and her eyes met mine and she nodded. The baby was gone.

They call it a miscarriage and it happens one time out of every five. That's what I read. Oh, maybe it happens more, maybe when the parents are like me and Elsa it happens every time. I never even saw Elsa after that. I was fired from my job at the Riverwood Retreat and in return for my silence on the matter my record stated only that I was terminated for personal differences, or something like that.

I'm a bit older now and I find myself wondering about the child that Elsa and I could have made. Children, I believe, can exceed the sum total of their parents. Perhaps in their little genes lie lessons learned from all of our past mistakes. We never could have raised that kid right, Elsa and I, but maybe she would still have grown up to be beautiful and strong.

TRAVELS WITH PAUL

had been fired from my job for a stupid indiscre-
tion and needed to leave town. I packed up my belongings
quickly and caught a ride with an acquaintance who was
headed out West. I say "acquaintance" because I'd only met him
once before. He was an Irish fellow named Paul O'Malley and he
was the cousin of a woman I used to date, or maybe they were
lovers, I don't know. She had introduced him to me one night in
a bar by saying, "This is my cousin Paul."

Paul was passing through town on his way to the West Coast
and had announced that he would be gone in the morning. I saw
him two weeks later though, right after I'd been fired from that
job. He was wandering downtown, looking a little dazed and
strung out.

"I haven't slept in three days," he told me.

"I thought you were going west," I said.

"I am."

"But you said you were leaving two weeks ago."

"I got hung up. Wait, two weeks? It hasn't been that long."

"Yes, it has."

"Oh." Paul scratched his head. His hair was thinning at the
top. He was a skinny guy with a long neck and an enormous
Adam's apple which bobbed up and down as he spoke. He needed

a shave too, or maybe he was growing a beard. The stubble was at that awkward scruffy halfway point.

"I got fired from my job," I told Paul. "I'd like to leave town."

"You want to ride with me? I'll leave tomorrow."

This idea seemed to perk Paul up. He clapped his hands together and rubbed his fuzzy chin.

"Sure, yeah, okay," I said.

"We'll leave in the morning."

"Great, fine."

We left two days later. Paul picked me up at my place, still looking tired and run-down.

"I can't sleep," he said. "I can't even shut my eyes."

"What's wrong with you?" I asked him.

"Nothing. Insomnia. I'm fine."

"You don't look fine."

"Well, I feel fine," he said, "I just can't sleep."

"Listen," I told him, "I don't want any funny business. I just need a ride out of town."

"Sure, right, I understand that," he said.

Paul's car was a small Ford hatchback. It was already crammed full with his stuff, so I had to leave several of my belongings behind. I left them at the house of a friend with the understanding that I'd return for them later. I never did.

Anyway, we hit the road and began our journey west. Paul's car was equipped with a set of very worn-out seats. The one I was sitting in, the passenger seat, had something wrong with the backrest. If I leaned back it would slope off to one side and I'd twist around uncomfortably. I'd been hoping to get a little sleep while he drove, but I could see now that this wouldn't be possible.

After about three hours of driving Paul pulled off the highway and stopped in front of a pizza shop. He unbuckled his pants and pulled them down to his knees. Then he looked at me.

"What are you doing?" I asked him.

"I thought maybe you'd like to give me a blow job," he said.

"No," I said. "No, I wouldn't."

Paul pursed his lips and nodded his head.

"All right," he said, pulling his pants up in a hurry. He put the car in gear and sped back out onto the highway.

Now things were awkward between us. We drove for a few hours in silence. A heavy rain began to fall as we crossed the state line into Ohio. When the big trucks passed by, water splashed against our windshield and threatened to push the little car right off the road. Paul had to jerk the steering wheel this way and that to keep us on course.

"Are you getting tired?" I asked Paul. "I can drive. I'm a good driver."

"That's okay," said Paul. "I like to drive."

But then a few minutes later he said, "Actually, I'm getting sick of this. Maybe you should take the wheel."

"Okay," I said.

He pulled over and we switched seats, running around opposite ends of the car quickly so as to not get too wet from the rain.

The driver's seat was even less comfortable than the passenger seat. I felt like I was sitting in a bucket. The little hatchback was difficult to operate as well. The clutch was loose and I was never quite sure when it would kick into gear. Out on the highway we continued to bob about like a rowboat on rough seas.

"I hope this rain stops soon," I told Paul.

"Oh, it will," he said.

Paul leaned back and tried to shut his eyes. Every time he did though, he could only keep them closed for a few seconds. Then he'd pop them open and his head would snap forward.

"What was that?" he'd ask me.

"Nothing," I'd say, "I'm just driving."

"I can't even take a nap," said Paul, finally. "This is a big pain in the ass."

"Maybe you should take some sleeping pills," I suggested.

"Oh, I won't do that," said Paul. "That's a vicious cycle. Everyone knows that."

"Okay," I said.

A while later Paul sat up and said, "Are you trying to kill me?"

"No," I said, "I'm not. I was trying to help."

Paul stared at me with his bloodshot eyes and I could see then that if he didn't get some sleep soon things were going to unravel.

"I'm pulling over," I told Paul. "Maybe I should get out."

"What do you mean?" he asked.

"I think I should get out here," I said. "I've gone far enough."

"What are you talking about?" said Paul. He rubbed his face and leaned forward in his seat. "You said you wanted to come west. We're only in Ohio."

"I know that," I told him. "I just think you need some sleep. We both do, actually."

"Well, that's fine, but don't abandon me here. We've got a long ways to go. I'm not doing this alone."

"You were going to do it alone before," I pointed out.

"Oh, don't pull that on me now," said Paul. He slapped his hand against the window. The rain was letting up, at least. I thought Paul was going to cry.

We passed by a sign for a town named Zanesville and Paul said, "Hey!"

"What?"

"I know someone in Zanesville."

"We passed it already."

"No, let's stop there. She's a nice gal. She'll give us food. I haven't seen her in years. She'll be happy to see me."

I wasn't so sure about that, but I thought this might be my chance to make a clean break, so I pulled off at the next exit and we backtracked to Zanesville. It was a muddy town situated on the bank of a river. Paul had me drive around in circles for over an hour looking for a street name with the word "Cherry" in it.

"Cherryvale. Cherryville, something like that."

When we found the street it was called VINE ST.

"Cherries grow on vines," explained Paul. "They're vegetables. They grow on vines."

After some more aimless driving along this street we stopped in front of a brown cottage with a mailbox shaped like a football.

"This is Alberta's house," said Paul. "This is it!"

"Are you sure? How do you know?"

"I was here before," he said. "I spent a week and a half here. I remember this place."

We walked up to the front door and Paul pounded upon it.

"We go way back, me and Alberta," Paul said to me. "We had a good thing going."

"When was this?" I asked.

"Six years ago," said Paul. "Or maybe seven. She'll remember me."

He knocked on the door again but it appeared that no one was home. Paul leaned over a hedge and looked through the window.

"Hmmm," he said. He tried turning the door handle but it was locked. He looked back in the window again.

"We shouldn't go in there," I said to him.

"I know, I know."

We sat down on the doorstep and watched the cars drive by. I had seen a bus station back in town when we were driving around. I thought maybe I could catch a ride over there and find a bus headed west.

"I think I'll head over to the bus station," I said to Paul.

"Oh no," he said. "Oh no, you don't. You haven't even met Alberta."

"She's not home," I pointed out. "She might not come back for days."

Paul thought about this for a moment. "She wouldn't do that," he said. "She wouldn't just disappear."

"You haven't seen her for six years," I said. "You have no idea what she might be up to."

"Look," Paul said, "do you trust me or not?"

I could have told him honestly that I did not. What kind of question was that? But instead I said, "I trust you, Paul."

We sat on the step for a while longer. Paul shut his eyes and rested his greasy head on my shoulder. I was afraid to move because I knew he needed sleep. We sat like that for perhaps twenty uncomfortable minutes and then a pickup truck rumbled to a stop in front of the house. Two teenagers, a boy and a girl, both overweight and pale, got out and began walking cautiously toward us. They were holding hands. I jiggled my shoulder and Paul opened his eyes.

"That's not Alberta," he said to me. He shut his eyes again.

"They're walking this way," I told him.

"So what?" said Paul. He refused to move.

The girl squinted at us and said something into her boyfriend's ear. They stopped walking and looked us over. The girl was wearing a lot of dark makeup around her eyes. She had dark lipstick on too. The boy had stringy black hair and was wearing a hefty pair of black boots affixed with many buckles. The two of them could have been dressed up for Halloween, but it wasn't that time of year.

It appeared that no one else was going to do any talking, so I said, "Hello."

"Hi," said the girl.

Paul still had his head resting on my shoulder and I pushed it off so that he would sit up. He rubbed at his eyes and blinked at the young couple in front of us.

"What the fuck happened to you two?" he said.

"I live here," said the girl.

"Here?" said Paul.

"Yes."

Paul stood up and turned around as if he didn't know there was a house behind him. I stood up too, trying to look apologetic.

"This is Alberta's house," Paul said.

"Right," said the girl. "She's my mother."

Paul eyed her skeptically. "Your mother? What's your name?"

"Linda," said the girl.

"Linda!" Paul cracked a smile and moved toward her. The girl stepped back, away from him. The boy shuffled uneasily in his enormous boots.

"I know your mother," Paul said to the girl. "And I know you too. I remember when you were just a little whippersnapper who wet her pants every morning. Remember that? You and me used to read the comics in the paper together. Boy, you've really grown up. Gotten fat, actually. It's me, Paul O'Malley, remember? What the fuck are you two doing to your faces anyway?"

Linda said, "I don't remember you."

"Sure you do," said Paul. "Seriously, what is that in your lip, a fishhook?" He was referring to a ring which Linda had stuck through her lip. The boy had one too, except it was stuck through his eyebrow.

"My mom's not home yet," said the girl. "She's at work. She gets home at eight."

"Great, no problem," said Paul. "We'll wait inside."

He stepped aside so that Linda could get by. Linda and the boyfriend walked past us and opened the door.

"Don't do anything stupid," said Linda. "My mom's boyfriend will kick your ass if you mess anything up."

"It's cool," said Paul. "I just want to take a nap."

The house was cluttered with various knickknacks, a lot of stuffed animals and products associated with the Cleveland Browns football team. We sat down in the living room and talked to the kids for a while. Linda's boyfriend was named Ryan. They went to school together and had been dating for about three months. Ryan pulled out a pipe and offered us some marijuana but Paul wouldn't touch it. He said it would keep him awake.

Linda and her boyfriend got bored with us and went into her bedroom and shut the door. Paul poured himself a glass of milk from the refrigerator, sat back down on the living room couch, and turned on the television.

"I'm going to leave now," I said.

"No fucking way," said Paul.

"Yes, I'm leaving."

"Just stay here until I fall asleep," he said. "I haven't slept in five days."

"Turn off the TV, then. Go to sleep."

Paul turned off the TV, drank his milk, and lay back on the couch. I was tired too and decided I could use a little rest. I lay down on the shag-carpeted floor and shut my eyes. Paul kept shifting about on the couch and cursing, so I found it hard to actually sleep. I kept thinking I heard Alberta coming and I would sit up, afraid she'd find us lying there and uncomfortable confusion would ensue.

A rhythmic thumping noise drifted out of Linda's bedroom and Paul said, "Hey, those kids are humping in there."

He jumped up and before I could stop him he was knocking on Linda's door, saying, "Stop that, you little rabbits!"

He burst through the door and indeed the two of them were naked, rolling about among the stuffed animals on her single bed.

Linda said, "Will you shut the door?"

Paul said, "Not until you get dressed!"

It was an uneasy standoff, but eventually Paul left them alone and lay back down on the couch. There was no more noise from Linda's room and I finally fell asleep on that shag-carpet floor. When I woke up, Paul was in the kitchen coughing and making a big racket. I went in there and he was kneeling on the floor with his head stuck in the oven. The room smelled like gas.

"What's going on here?" I asked.

"Fuck," said Paul. "Shit."

He was trying to inhale the gas fumes in order to kill himself but he couldn't create a proper seal around his head, so the gas escaped into the room. I grabbed his legs and pulled him away from the oven.

"Leave me alone!" he cried out.

We wrestled about on the kitchen floor and during the struggle Paul tried to kiss me, his hairy face and puckered lips lunging out my way.

"I'm not a gay," he said. "I can't sleep. Just kiss me."

Finally I got him to calm down and we sat together on the linoleum floor breathing heavily, sucking in that gas-filled air.

"I've got a headache," said Paul.

There was a clicking sound from Linda's room and then a warm blue flame rushed across the hallway floor and burst into the kitchen with a loud hot boom. For a brief second the whole room filled up with a wall of fire and then suddenly we were sitting in the charred kitchen with little flames flickering around us. The paper towels were burning, and so were some pot holders and the curtains. Paul and I stood up and slapped at the flames and threw water everywhere. Ryan came in and helped us. We yanked the curtains down and tossed them in the sink. A smoke alarm went off and its shrill noise drove us nuts until Paul swatted it down with a broom. After a while we managed to put out all the fires in the house. The shag carpet was seared black and some of the stuffed animals were still smoking. Linda sat crying in her bedroom. The place smelled awful now, like burnt plastic. Paul and I noticed that our hair was singed too. Our eyebrows were mostly gone and the skin on our faces was red and burned.

"We could have died," said Paul.

"That was your goal," I reminded him. "You had your head in the oven."

Ryan apologized because it was his lighter which had set off the flame.

"That's what you get for smoking those doobies, you little fornicator," said Paul.

"I'm sorry," said Ryan. He was really shaken up. We all were.

It was nearly eight o'clock and Alberta would soon be coming home. Paul decided maybe she wouldn't be so happy to see him after all. He and I had a brief discussion away from the kids and then we dashed out to his little hatchback and drove away, leaving Linda and Ryan to explain the mess we'd left behind.

"That Linda has really changed," said Paul. "I remember when she was just a cute small girl. Now look at her, all painted up and punched full of metal."

A police car passed us going the other way, its lights flashing and siren blaring. Paul began to get paranoid and insisted that we ditch the car. That was fine with me.

We parked the car on a side street and walked over to the bus station, where we purchased two tickets to Seattle, a thirty-seven-hour ride. As we waited for the bus to show up Paul lay down across three of those plastic bus stop seats and he finally fell asleep. It was chilly in there and those seats looked about as comfortable as a pile of rocks, but there he was, snoring away. I briefly considered waking him up when the bus arrived and they announced that it was time for us to load on, but then I thought better of it. He was still sleeping like a baby, curled up contentedly under those pale fluorescent lights, when we pulled away and headed west without him.

The real estate agent who sold me the house had mentioned the box only in passing.

"There's a structure in the backyard," she told me. "You can't move it. It's an eminent domain thing, grandfathered in. But it won't bother you."

I examined the box more closely later on, before finalizing the purchase. It was about eight feet square, and made of gray, weathered steel, a generic box if there ever was one. I was informed that it was a "transfer box" and inside of it were a set of circuits involved in the underground conduction of electricity. The rusted bolt lock at the base seemed like it hadn't been opened for years.

"Can I cover it up with vegetation?" I inquired.

The response took three days to arrive and it was, "No."

But the house was inexpensive and located on the side of a pleasant hill, unobservable by my neighbors, a feature which I liked. I wasn't up to anything covert, mind you, I just enjoy solitude, and the notion that I might do something like stroll about in my home naked without feeling self-conscious pleased me. In truth I rarely did that.

Earlier that year I'd lost my foot in a wood-chipper accident. I had negotiated a lump payment from the county, with whom I was employed when it happened, and this was how I paid for the house. It goes without saying I would have preferred to keep my foot instead of that house, but I wasn't entirely displeased with the arrangement. A house for a foot. Worse deals have been struck.

It was during the winter that I first began to notice the heat emanating from the box. A heavy snow had fallen overnight and in the morning I went out for a walk with my dog. Everything was white and pillowy except for that box. It was bare and steam rose from its steel casing. I touched it and nearly burned my fingertips. Later on, I noticed the snow on the ground around the box had begun to melt away as well. By day's end there was a muddy brown circle, like a moat, surrounding it. I called the power company and was bounced around several different departments before they agreed to send a crew over.

The crew arrived and stared at the box.

"It's just a box," they said to me. "It isn't one of ours. We don't even know what's inside of it."

"Well, can you open it up?" I asked. "I'm concerned about the heat."

"No, sir," said the foreman, "we're not allowed to interfere with this kind of thing. Liability. I suggest you figure out who put this here."

I called the fire department and by the time they got to my place the box had cooled down.

"Let us know if it starts heating up again," said the fire chief. "Or get it fixed."

"I don't even know what it is," I said.

The real estate agent who sold me the house put me in touch with the town zoning commission, who were the ones who thought it belonged to the power company. Apparently I had signed something attached to the deed and title in which I agreed to leave that box untouched, but no one was sure who had put it there. The previous owner of the house was dead and, like me, had valued solitude. The box didn't heat up like that again though, and after a few days I was tempted to forget about it.

My closest neighbors were two women known as the Harper sisters. They lived together in the same run-down farmhouse where they had been born. They grew marijuana on the property and raised a breed of cat known as Manx cats, meaning they had no tails. Suzette, the eldest sister, was over six feet tall and quite skinny. I was afraid of her. Lila, the younger one, wasn't so tall and smiled a lot. She had a large gap between her two front teeth, which was not unattractive.

Shortly after the box had cooled down Lila showed up at my front door looking for one of her cats.

"His name is Sinclair," she told me. "He's friendly and doesn't usually wander. Has he been around here?"

"I haven't seen him," I told her. "Listen, do you know anything about the metal box in my backyard? It was giving off steam when it snowed a few days ago."

"Steam?" said Lila.

"Well, heat," I said. "I suppose it was just the snow that turned to steam."

Lila walked around back with me and together we looked at the box.

"Seems like government work to me," she said. "I'd be happy to help you bury it. Suzette could bring over the tractor and knock it down."

"Well, I'm not sure I should do that," I said. "I was told it wasn't technically my property."

"Who told you that?"

"I don't know," I said.

Lila gazed down at my prosthetic foot. The prosthesis ended below my knee, but she couldn't see that. Perhaps she wondered just how far up it went.

"You're doing pretty well on that thing," she told me.

"Thanks," I said. "I'll keep an eye out for your cat."

A few weeks later I was awakened by a shrill hissing sound, like a large distressed bird had entered my home. I thought perhaps some appliance had sprung a leak. But after a quick examination I determined the sound was coming from outside, from the box.

I grabbed a maul from the woodshed and slammed it against the box several times. This didn't help anything. I tried going back to sleep but it wasn't possible with that noise. I considered driving my car up there and crashing it into the box, but, before I could do that, the hissing stopped.

In the morning I paid a visit to the Harper sisters to see about taking Lila up on her offer to plow over the box with their tractor. Lila and Suzette were sitting at the kitchen table trimming dried-out marijuana plants with a group of teenagers.

"Did you find my cat?" asked Lila.

"No," I told her. "He's still gone?"

"We think he died," said Suzette.

"You think he died," corrected Lila. "I think he's gone rogue."

"Well, I'm wondering if you might be able to bring your tractor over to my place this afternoon," I said. "That metal box started hissing last night and I couldn't sleep. I was hoping you could knock it over and bury it."

"That's a bad idea," said Suzette.

"I'll bring the tractor over at two o'clock," said Lila.

We all smoked some of their marijuana, which was very strong because it had been grown indoors using seeds shipped from engineers in Holland. One of the teenagers, a guy named Alf, turned out to be Suzette's son. This surprised me because she didn't seem old enough to have birthed a teenager, an older teenager at that. He had a beard.

Two o'clock rolled around and none of us had moved from the kitchen.

"Time to get that tractor," said Lila, punching me in the arm.

Alf volunteered to help with the box-demolition project and another fellow whose name I've forgotten agreed to come along as well. We ventured out to the barn where the tractor was kept and Alf and his friend refused to put on coats despite the cold weather. They were tough, punk-rock-type guys who didn't appear to bathe much, if at all.

First we had to dig out the area around the barn door because it hadn't been opened since the big snowfall. Then Lila opened up the door and Alf set to work starting up the tractor. It had been sitting there all winter and needed some coaxing. I began poking around the barn looking for a length of chain, which might come in handy if we decided to tow the box away. I peered down into a barrel and discovered Sinclair, the missing cat. He was dead.

"Aw, fuck, he must have gotten stuck in there," said Lila.

She was upset and the work on the tractor was forgotten. Instead we dug a grave out in the small meadow where they buried their animals. This was hard work because the ground was mostly frozen and we had to use pickaxes. Alf wondered if we might wait until spring, but Lila said that was disrespectful.

Suzette came outside for the burial and expressed the opinion that Sinclair was an old cat and had probably just been looking for a quiet place to die. At first this further agitated Lila, but then she began to take some solace in the notion that Sinclair might not have been struggling and calling out for help. From the looks of his frozen body, he had been in there for quite a while.

Alf's friend said he had examined the barrel where I'd discovered Sinclair and had seen a mouse skeleton in there as well.

"I bet the cat was chasing after that mouse," he said.

"So at least he had something to eat," observed Alf. But then he trailed off on this thought as Lila once again began to cry.

"Why don't the two of you shut the fuck up?" said Suzette.

We buried the cat and agreed to take on the box project the next day. This was just as well, because when I got home there was a van parked in front of my house and a group of men in white jumpsuits were gathered around the box. I was glad to see people in an official-looking capacity taking interest in it.

"Are you the owners of this box?" I called out to them as I approached.

A small fellow stepped forward and introduced himself as Dr. Cox. "Have you been striking this container?" he asked.

I noticed there were several large dents on the sides where I'd gone at it with the maul the night before.

"It was making a terrible noise," I told him. "It also got very hot during the snowstorm. Steam was coming off of it and I thought it might explode."

"So you beat upon it with a stick?" said Dr. Cox.

"I used a maul," I said. "And I didn't hit it until the noise came out. I couldn't sleep. Who are you people anyway?"

There was a pause as Dr. Cox glanced back at his cohorts. One of them stepped forward and handed me a business card that was crowded with words.

"We're with NOAA," he said. "And we're going to ask that you refrain from abusing this device."

"I don't know what NOAA is," I said.

"Look it up," said Dr. Cox. "We've made some adjustments to the device, nothing which concerns you, of course."

"It does concern me," I said. "I live here. It keeps making noise and heating up."

"That shouldn't happen anymore," said Dr. Cox. "We appreciate you bringing it to our attention."

With that, Dr. Cox signaled to his team and they followed him as he walked past me, down the hill, and toward the van. I noticed that the rusted lock on the box's door had been replaced. I tried to peer down through the small vents to see what was going on inside, but it was dark.

"You're leaving now?" I called out to the white-coated men. "I'd just like to know what this box is for."

"Read the notice on your door," said Dr. Cox. And with that they all piled into the van and left.

The notice on my door was written on letterhead from the National Oceanic and Atmospheric Administration. So that was what "NOAA" stood for. It said, in so many words, that the box belonged to them and it had something to do with the monitoring of atmospheric conditions. It was full of "highly sensitive instruments." I was forbidden to "interfere with or molest it further," under penalty of law.

Baffled, but also somewhat impressed at the newfound importance of my backyard, I called up the Harper sisters. Suzette laughed at my news.

"Good thing you dumbasses didn't go and knock it over," she said.

Lila was mad though. "Classic government claptrap," she said.

A few days passed during which the box and I coexisted peaceably, and then, one night, I spotted the shafts of light. They flickered through the vents in the box's sides. At first I assumed it was sparks, signs of an impending combustion, and I prepared to leave the premises. But then I saw that it was simply light, a steady stream peeking out from within. I crept up next to the box and was very surprised to hear what sounded like voices coming from inside. People! Underground! There was a group of them down there occupying some cavern to which this box was merely an entrance. For so long I had thought it was just a box!

I listened for some time to what they were saying. What I could make out was mostly mundane stuff, arguments about the score of some board game they were playing, a dispute over what they might eat for dinner and how best to prepare it. They had a kitchen down there!

I decided I had had enough. I banged on the box and yelled down to them, "Hey! This is my property! You can't live under-neath my ground! Come out of there!"

There was a quick silence, much the way crickets immedi-ately cease their chirping at the first sign of an intruder. The lights inside clicked off.

"Hello?" I called down to them. "Open up this box! I want to see what's down there!"

Again, I received no reply. I banged on the box repeatedly and kicked at it with my prosthetic foot.

"Answer me!" I called out. "I heard you talking!"

They were strong-willed though, whoever they were, and they sat quietly in the darkness for a long time. I began to wonder if I'd somehow imagined their presence, if perhaps I was going in-sane living out here on my own. I got up and stumbled home.

When I told Lila Harper about the voices and the lights I'd seen she came over to my place with a steel cable and a lock.

"We're going to lock those fuckers in," she told me.

I liked this idea, though I was wary of Dr. Cox and his orders not to molest the box. Lila had no fear of NOAA, however.

"You think we need a government agency to tell us what the weather is?" she said. "It's mind control, Georgie. I knew there was something creepy about that box. It's typical of them to pick on a man with only one foot. You can blame it all on me if they come after you," she said.

It was exhilarating to see Lila so worked up over this. I'd come across several antigovernment types in my travels up to that point. They all had their favorite conspiracies, but rarely did they ever have the chance to see their paranoia manifest before them. I helped Lila affix the lock and cable so that the box could not be opened. Then Lila smacked the side of the box with a hammer and yelled down through the vents, "We've locked you assholes in! You're stuck!"

She laughed, and for some time there was no response from inside the box. But then, just as we were about to walk away, there came a tapping sound from inside. The tapping grew louder and more frantic and then became a series of loud bangs.

"Can't get out, can you?" Lila said to the box.

"Hey," said a timid voice from inside. "Did you really lock us in?"

"You know it!" said Lila.

"Well," said the voice, "that hardly seems fair."

"This is my property," I told the voice. "You all trespassed across my property in order to get in there. You tell your buddy Dr. Cox I'm filing a complaint."

"Dr. Cox is a moron," said the voice from inside.

Both Lila and I were a little taken aback by this response. We'd thought of NOAA as a unified front.

"Well," I said, "how about you tell Dr. Cox to come retrieve you and your friends and get the hell off my property?"

"Now, see here," said the voice, "we are currently dwelling underground, well below the jurisdiction of your property lines. And besides, the Department of Commerce has declared a right of passage, upholdable by federal law."

"Department of Commerce?" said Lila.

"Of which NOAA is a division," said the voice.

"We're going back inside my house," I told him. "You all have a fun time down there doing whatever it is you are doing."

"It's an ion study!" cried the voice. "Very important research."

"Come on," said Lila. "Let's go."

She invited me back to her place, where we sat in the kitchen and smoked marijuana while the Manx cats scampered over the counters and tables.

"How come they don't have tails?" I asked Lila.

"They come from the Isle of Man," she told me. "Where the wild cats bred with the rabbits."

Suzette walked in and said, "That's not true. That's a myth."

"I've been to the Isle of Man," said Lila, "and the people there confirm it's true."

"Don't cats need their tails for balance?" I asked. "How come these cats don't fall over?"

"That's a silly question," said Suzette, "especially from a guy with one leg."

"I have two legs," I told her. "Just not two feet."

Then Alf came running in saying I should move my car into the barn because a big storm was coming.

"They say it's going to drop two feet of snow."

"I should go home, then," I said. "What about the people in the box?"

"They weren't going anywhere anyway," said Lila, and I agreed with her.

I parked my car inside the big barn, next to the tractor which we had never used. I didn't believe the storm would amount to much, but Suzette said she could feel its severity in her bones.

It started snowing and strong winds began to howl through the trees. I had been hoping Lila would invite me upstairs to spend the night with her but instead she pulled out some blankets and offered me the couch. Suzette's bones were right about the storm. It was big and strong, and I slept well with the snow swirling about outside. One of the cats curled up and wedged itself behind my knees.

The storm didn't let up until past noon the next day. It was a doozy, covering the ground in a heavy blanket of snow and knocking over several trees on the Harper sisters' land. The snow had built up so thickly on top of their old barn that the roof caved in and we had to dig out my car and the old tractor too. The general digging out took a long time and I couldn't get back to my house until the following day. Lila came with me when I did return and we were surprised to find that a large tree had crashed down upon the box. The metal structure had been ripped from the concrete foundation and now it lay flipped on its side, covered in snow. There was just a hole where it once stood, with a ladder leading down to the world below. Together Lila and I explored the cavern. It was like a submarine down there, a hallway of rooms filled with old instruments and dusty computers. The people were gone. Signs of a hasty exit were evident, half-packed bags, unfinished food in the refrigerator. Had Dr. Cox come to their rescue in the middle of the storm?

We thought the place was empty but then we heard a little *meow*. Lila ventured down a hallway and discovered her lost cat, Sinclair, lying happily on a bunk bed.

"Sinclair!" she exclaimed, her eyes welling up with tears. "Sinclair, it's you. I knew it. It is you."

I was confused, of course, because I had been under the impression we had buried Sinclair some weeks earlier.

"That must have been another cat," said Lila. "This one here is Sinclair. I'm sure of it."

They certainly did seem to know each other, this cat and Lila. She stroked his ears and kissed him, while he purred loudly and kneaded his paws into her lap.

"Perhaps he was reincarnated," I suggested.

"Perhaps," said Lila. "I've heard of that happening to Manx cats from time to time. They are an ancient breed."

Surely Suzette would have another explanation, but I for one was willing to accept some of this logic. Who knows what can come of breeding cats and rabbits on some faraway island? Who really knows the power of the great winter storms?

I heard no more from Dr. Cox and his scientist buddies at NOAA. They abandoned their ion study, I suppose. Or maybe they had learned all they sought to know. They say NOAA can control the weather now, that there are satellites roaming the skies with giant mirrors, and certain airplanes seed the clouds with chemicals unfamiliar to us civilians down below. It's all for our benefit, they say, a great equalization of the rampant forces we've unleashed upon nature. We have to do it, they say, otherwise we won't survive the changes to come.

SNAKEBITE

We were riding in a car together, Clifford, his wife, Jolene, and I. Clifford was at the wheel and Jolene sat next to him, up front. I was in the back. We were running late, on our way to the wedding of a friend named Margaret out in the hills of Virginia. According to Jolene, I was underdressed. I had neglected to bring a tie and, instead of shoes, I was wearing a pair of sneakers.

"You look like a jackass," said Jolene.

"It's a country wedding," I said. "This is appropriate."

Clifford refused to weigh in on the subject, but I did notice he was wearing a tie and some nicely polished shoes. I wondered if maybe someone at the wedding might have an extra tie which I could slip on before the ceremony. There probably wasn't time for that though. I could put the tie on afterward, but then everyone would know that I was just taking action after the fact. I looked down at my ratty sneakers and realized Jolene was probably right. I looked like a jackass.

We were driving on a country road and it was spring, a sunny April day in the mountains. Clifford sped along trying to make up for lost time. The hillsides were green and popping with little white flowers. There were some yellow ones out there too. Even a person like me, poorly dressed and feeling glum about it, could appreciate the beauty of the day.

Jolene said, "Look at this weather. Margaret's a lucky gal. Well, about the weather anyway."

Jolene was not fond of Margaret's husband-to-be. He was a lanky plumber's assistant from Culpeper named Luke. I liked him fine, though months earlier I'd actually advised him not to get married. He had confided in me one night that he was thinking about proposing to Margaret and I told him that they didn't seem as if they were ready for that. The very next day Luke bought a ring from the pawnshop and got down on his knee. That's how much my advice was worth to him. Jolene felt that Luke was a "simpleton."

The wedding was set to take place at a farm. We were about twenty minutes away, nearly there, when we came upon a plump man waving his arms in the middle of the road. His vehicle, an older-model Cadillac, was pulled off to the side, and one of his pants legs was rolled up to his knee.

"Don't stop," said Jolene. "We'll be late."

"I have to stop," said Clifford. "He's waving."

"Drive around him."

Clifford slowed down and tried to coast by slowly but the man flung himself onto the hood of our car. Clifford hit the brakes and the man just lay there on his belly, breathing heavily.

"Get off!" yelled Jolene.

"I think there's something wrong with him," I said.

"Good observation," said Jolene. "Speed up, Cliff. We're late as it is."

"Don't do that," I said.

Clifford was trying to think things over. The man on the hood lifted his head and gazed at us through the windshield, his round face covered in sweat. He had a little brown mustache perched above his small, thin-lipped mouth.

"Help me," he said to us.

"Oh Jesus," said Jolene.

I sensed an opportunity here to make myself useful. I opened up my door and got out to confront this fellow.

"What's going on here?" I asked him.

The chubby man pointed down toward his ankle, the one with the cuff rolled up. "I got bit," he said, wincing. "Snakebite."

I stepped forward and examined the spot on his leg. There were indeed two red small holes, fang marks, I suppose, where a snake, or some other small animal, had struck him. It didn't look like anything very serious to me.

"Does it hurt?" I asked.

"Oh God, yes!" said the man. "I think my leg's gone numb."

Jolene leaned her head out the window and said, "Tell this person to please get off our car."

The man gave Jolene a pitiful look and slowly rolled off the hood, landing gingerly on his one good leg.

"We're late for a wedding," I explained to him.

"I think I've been poisoned," said the man. "I could really use some help. I can't drive like this. My leg's nearly paralyzed."

"What did the snake look like?" I asked.

"It had stripes and some colors on its head. A little guy. Those are supposed to be the worst kind, the little ones. Right?"

"What color was its head?" I didn't know much about snakes, but this seemed like a sensible question.

"Orange, I think. Or red. Maybe white."

"Get in the car, Georgie," Jolene said to me. "We're leaving."

The snake-bitten man gazed at me with beady, helpless eyes. They were like two raisins set in a mound of dough. "Don't leave me here," he said. "I'll die."

Clifford honked his horn and lurched forward.

"Please," said the man.

I made an executive decision just then. "Hop in," I said. "We'll find a doctor at the wedding."

Jolene was disgusted at this development and told Clifford to hit the gas and ditch us both before we could climb in the car. Clifford saw no way out of it though, and waited until we'd gotten inside before he began to drive. Jolene shook her head and muttered curse words as we picked up speed. She remained unconvinced of our passenger's plight even after we showed her the fang marks on his ankle.

"It looks like you got bit by a mouse. Are you sure it wasn't a mouse? Or a rat?"

"I'm sure, madam," said the man. His name was Willis Cotcher. He told us he was on his way to visit a lady acquaintance a few hours south and had stepped out of his car to relieve himself when, as he put it, "the serpent struck."

"Serpent, my ass," said Jolene. "I don't believe this shit. We can't just bring a stranger to Margaret's wedding."

"He's dressed for it," I pointed out.

This was true. Willis was wearing a light blue suit and, I noted with envy, a sporty tie. I thought about asking him if I could borrow it, but I would have felt badly about putting him at even more of a disadvantage. I realized too late that I should have asked if he had another tie back in his car. That way I could have put it on as we were driving.

Willis twisted about in the cramped backseat and began to moan.

"My leg," he said. "It feels like it's full of sand. I can't look at it. Is it turning blue?"

Willis lifted up his leg and it was indeed a little blue. There was a bruise developing around the two holes in his ankle.

"Oh wow," I said.

Willis's face got pale. "I'm going to vomit," he said.

"Oh, you'd better not," said Jolene.

"I might faint," said Willis. "I feel dizzy."

Clifford spoke up. "What shape was its head?"

"Its head?" asked Willis. "Do you mean the snake's head?"

"Right," said Clifford. "Was it shaped like a triangle?"

"You mean pointy? Yes. Yes, I believe it was. Is that bad?"

"What about its eyes. Were they colored?"

"They were green. Or maybe yellow."

"Sounds like a cottonmouth to me," said Clifford.

"Is that bad?"

"Well, it's not good."

"Oh Lord," said Willis. "I can't feel my leg at all. Am I paralyzed?"

Right as he said that Willis lifted up his leg and moved it around.

"It's not paralyzed," I said.

"We need a knife," said Clifford. "Cut an X over the snakebite and suck the poison out."

"What?"

"That's what you're supposed to do. It's in the *Boy Scout Handbook*. You suck out the poison."

"Who sucks out the poison?"

"You," said Clifford, looking back at me. Willis looked at me too. He was sweating profusely now, nodding his pudgy head.

"I'd be most appreciative," he said.

Clifford opened up the glove compartment and fished out a small penknife. He handed it to me.

"Here you go," he said.

I turned to Jolene for some sort of confirmation that this was a poor idea, but she seemed through with the matter.

"Don't look at me," she said. "You're the dumbass who let him in the car. Go ahead and suck on his foot. Maybe it'll help." She cracked a smile when she said that. This was amusing her, apparently. I took the knife from Clifford and flipped open the blade.

"Cut deep enough so that you draw blood," said Clifford. "That way you'll get most of the poison out when you suck on it."

"Is this safe?" I asked.

Willis was beginning to shake. "Don't worry," he said, "I can take it."

"I mean the blood," I said. "Is it safe for me to suck on blood? How far are we from the wedding? Maybe I should wait."

Clifford said, "Don't wait another minute. Every second counts when you're dealing with venom."

So now Clifford was an expert on this subject. In all the years I'd known him I'd never once heard him discuss snake venom. Willis trembled some more and pushed his beefy leg onto my lap.

"Please, Georgie," he said to me. "I don't want to die. Just get it out, please."

I sized up the spot and tried to hold his leg steady. Clifford slowed down a little and turned to look back as I made the cut. The knife was not as sharp as one would like for such an operation. I had to press down pretty hard just to break the skin. Willis let out an anguished howl.

"Oh Jesus!" he cried.

I was making a mess of it. Instead of a neat X I carved a set of short ugly gouges around the two original tooth marks left by "the serpent."

"Quickly," said Clifford, "suck it!"

Little curly hairs sprouted up from Willis's beefy leg. He was pretty much sobbing from the pain now, and sweating like a hog. His leg felt like a big wet sponge.

"That blood's going to stain your pants," said Jolene.

SNAKEBITE

This was true. A line of blood trickled down Willis's calf and into my lap. I wiped it away with my hand, and then leaned down and shut my eyes. I placed my lips on Willis's leg and sucked his salty, musky blood into my mouth. I tried not to taste it, but as soon as it hit my tongue I began to gag. I kept myself there for just a moment longer, to preserve the appearance that I was still extracting something, and then I popped my head up and spit Willis's blood out the car window. It dribbled against the side of the car in a string of red slime.

"Turn here," said Jolene.

We'd arrived at the wedding. What an entrance! Clifford pulled the car into the middle of a bumpy meadow where everyone else had parked. Willis sat there heaving and mopping sweat from his brow. Clifford handed him a handkerchief and told him not to let his blood get on the car seat.

"Did you get all the poison out?" Willis asked me.

"I don't know," I said. "Sure. I got it. I think I did."

"Maybe you should try again," said Willis.

"I got most of it," I said. "I'm pretty sure."

Jolene stepped out of the car and said, "Damn it, we're late. Come on, Cliff, the ceremony's already started."

Clifford looked at the two of us, me underdressed, and now stained with blood, and Willis panting dramatically in the backseat.

"We'll find a doctor at the wedding," said Clifford. "You wait here, Mr. Cotcher. Come on, Georgie."

I got out of the car and tried to smooth out my clothes. There was a big spot of blood on my thigh and some smaller ones on my shirt. I ducked my head back in the car.

"Excuse me, Willis?" I said. "Do you think I could borrow your tie, just for the ceremony?"

Willis looked very put out by this request. I would have felt badly about asking except that I'd just sucked poison out of his leg. Plus his blood had ruined my clothes. It seemed like a reasonable trade. Willis begrudgingly loosened his tie and placed it in my hand.

"I'm leaving," said Jolene.

"You should try to relax," Clifford said to Willis. "The less your heart pumps, the less the poison can spread."

"What?" said Willis.

Jolene grabbed Clifford and the two of them walked away.

"My leg's still numb," said Willis.

"We'll find a doctor," I told him. And then I added, "A good one," hoping that this would make him feel better. I trotted off across the meadow to catch up with Clifford and Jolene.

The ceremony was well under way, like Jolene had said. Everyone was sitting outside on hay bales facing the bride and groom. As we got closer we could hear the preacher saying something about the long journey they were about to embark upon together.

Jolene was mortified. "I can't believe we're late for this," she said.

"We didn't miss the vows," I pointed out. I was trying to get my tie on as we walked.

"Who do we know here that's a doctor?" asked Clifford.

Jolene said, "Clifford, you are not going to disrupt Margaret's wedding to find a doctor for that idiot. He'll be just fine."

Clifford thought about this and, predictably, deferred to Jolene's judgment. We sat down in the back row just as our friend Amanda stood up front and began to play something on her accordion. Luke looked out over the assembled guests and swallowed deeply. He appeared pale and unhappy. Margaret's face was stern and resolute. She looked nice in her white dress though. And there were flowers in her hair.

Amanda shut her eyes and swayed back and forth with the slow rhythm of whatever hymn it was she was playing on that accordion. The song was interminable. People began to shift about on their hay bales and look at their watches. We were all sweltering under the sun and I became increasingly worried about Willis back there in the car.

Finally the preacher stepped forward and made Amanda stop. She nodded and took a seat. The preacher smiled out at us and remarked at what a handsome crowd we were. Everyone chuckled. This process was taking forever. I can never understand why they always drag a wedding out like that. We all couldn't wait to get out of the sun and find the bar. It occurred to me that if Willis were to die now I would have sucked on his leg for nothing.

The preacher backed up and took the hands of Margaret and Luke into his. He was a bit of a hippie, this preacher, with his stringy gray hair pulled back in a tight ponytail behind his head. He wanted everyone to join in on the blessing. We were supposed to channel good energy toward them, or something like that. I looked out toward the car and saw that Willis had gotten up from the backseat. He was standing there propped up against the car with his head resting in his hands. He peered over in our direction and then began limping awkwardly across the field. His bad leg moved stiffly, as if it were wrapped up in a cast. Eventually Willis fell down, face-first, and did not get up.

The preacher was about to proclaim Margaret and Luke man and wife, but first he asked us all, "Does anyone present know of a good reason why this couple should not be married here, before God? Speak now, or forever hold your peace."

There was a long, uncomfortable silence while people adjusted themselves again on those scratchy hay bales. Amanda stood up and strapped on her accordion, preparing to drone through another hymn. Willis was still lying out there on his face and I couldn't stand it any longer. I took advantage of the silence and called out, "Is anyone here a doctor?"

The entire gathering jerked their heads around and glared at me.

"I'm sorry," I said. "I have no objection to the marriage. Sorry about that. I just need to borrow a doctor. It's urgent. There's a man out in the meadow who got bit by a snake. His leg is numb."

Somebody called out, "Was its head triangle-shaped?"

I guess that was a standard question. I said we thought that perhaps it was. Someone asked if there was a rattle on its tail and I said I didn't know for sure, but thought not. An older gentleman from up front got to his feet and walked toward me.

"I'm a doctor," he said. It was Margaret's grandfather, Mr. Fiske. He was actually a veterinarian, and he had retired a few years ago, but this was no time to be picky.

"I'll be right back," Mr. Fiske said to his family. "Go on without me."

Jolene shot me a look of extreme contempt. "You son of a bitch," she whispered.

Clifford stared down at his feet. Mr. Fiske hobbled up the aisle, trying to move as quickly as he could.

"We'll be right back," I promised. "I'm sorry for the disturbance."

Waves of confusion washed over Luke's face. Margaret bit her lip and prepared to soldier on. Mr. Fiske and I hustled out to the meadow and left all that behind us. I heard the preacher say, "Now, where were we?" and there were a few forced chuckles from the guests.

"I'm sorry about this, Mr. Fiske," I said. "I feel awful for pulling you away."

"It's all right," said Mr. Fiske. "I was falling asleep. I'm afraid Margaret's chosen a retard boy for a husband."

"He's not so bad," I said.

"I didn't say he was bad," said Mr. Fiske, "just slow. Now, where is this sick person?"

"He's right out here," I said.

We soon came upon Willis lying facedown in the grass. I was worried he had expired, but then I saw his large body rise and fall with labored breaths.

"What's gotten into him?" asked Mr. Fiske.

"He's been poisoned," I said. "Or he thinks he has."

Mr. Fiske pushed at Willis's fleshy side with the tip of his shoe. "Wake up," he said.

Willis stirred a little and lifted his head. "Is it a doctor?" he asked. "Am I dead?"

Mr. Fiske looked at me. "Where did you find this fellow?"

"He was standing by the road back there," I said. "He got out of his car to relieve himself and something bit him. See, look at his leg."

The spot on Willis's leg was a bloody mess on account of my handiwork with the knife.

"A snake did that?" asked Mr. Fiske.

"No," I said. "I cut an X over the bite mark and sucked some of the poison out."

Mr. Fiske's face twisted up like he'd just eaten a lemon. "What the hell did you do that for?"

"It's in the *Boy Scout Handbook*."

"That organization is run by a bunch of lunatics. Lunatics and homosexuals. Did you know that?"

"I didn't know that," I said. "Clifford thinks it was a cottonmouth that bit him."

Willis rolled over and gazed up at us. "Am I dead? Am I going to die?"

Mr. Fiske shook his head. "No, son. No, you're not." He called everyone "son," no matter what their age. Willis here was probably fifty years old. Mr. Fiske pulled a silver flask from his breast pocket, unscrewed the cap, and splashed some of the liquor on Willis's wound. Willis screamed.

"Oh, it stings!"

"I bet it does," said Mr. Fiske. He took a nip from the flask and then passed it to me. "You better have some of this too, after sucking on that boy's leg."

I touched the flask to my lips and it made them tingle. The liquor went down like hot syrup.

"White lightning," said Mr. Fiske. "Disinfectant." He took back the flask and splashed a little more on Willis's leg. Then he made Willis take a swig himself.

"Whoa," said Willis, after drinking it down. "What was that? Is that medicine? Are you a doctor?"

"I'm a veterinarian," said Mr. Fiske. "And you'll be just fine. Quit your whining and get out of the sun."

We helped Willis to his feet and sat him down under a tree. Mr. Fiske gave him another hit off the flask and then told him to try to go to sleep. The ceremony was over now and we walked back to congratulate the new couple.

"Is he really going to be all right?" I asked Mr. Fiske.

"Sure he is."

Mr. Fiske and I each took one last nip from the silver flask and then he placed it back into his coat pocket.

By the time we returned, most of the guests had made a beeline for the bar. It was a hard-drinking crowd and that lengthy ceremony hadn't helped things. A few people commented on the blood on my outfit, and I had to readjust my tie and button up my coat. No one seemed too concerned about Willis's condition. Luke's father, a wiry little fellow with strange, leathery skin, told me he had chopped the head off a rattlesnake with an axe one time. When he went to fetch the skull as a souvenir, the detached head bit him right on the hand, "just like in *Old Yeller*."

I didn't remember that part of *Old Yeller*, but I told him it was a remarkable story. I asked him if he'd cut an X mark over the bite and sucked out the poison.

"Everybody knows that trick don't work," he said. Everyone but Clifford and me.

I went to find Clifford, but he was busy with Jolene and I didn't want to encounter her ire. A bluegrass band started up and people hooted as Margaret and Luke danced around in front of us. Luke got dizzy and had to sit down. Margaret's father took over and he tried to get the band to slow the tempo but they wouldn't. Then the rest of us joined in and whooped it up until dinner.

I brought a plate of barbeque over to Willis but he was still asleep under the tree where we'd left him. He was breathing and appeared okay, so I placed the plate of food beside him and went back to the festivities.

As dinner wound down Luke got up and told us all to be quiet. He held up his glass and said, "This is the most important day of my life, so far. I never thought I'd get married. It just wasn't something I thought I'd want to do. But Margaret here convinced me it was a good idea, and, well, we'll see how it goes."

Then he got out a guitar and played a Willie Nelson song, "To All the Girls I've Loved Before."

Margaret got up and said she didn't know what to say after that. "I know some of you think Luke isn't good enough for me, but you don't know him the way I do. He's a good man."

Jolene was crying but I wasn't sure about what. Clifford decided to stand up and make a speech as well.

"You two are a real inspiration, and I know you're going to be very happy," he said. "Those of us who are married already really appreciate it when our friends get hitched too, because now we're all in it together . . . What I mean to say is, if you stick with it, you will find rewards. Really. Don't get divorced, especially if you have children . . ."

Jolene hissed at Clifford and told him to sit down. She pinched me and said I should go up there and retrieve him, but I was wary of making another spectacle of myself. Clifford rambled on a little while longer. He told us about how he and Jolene had been trying to have kids but he thought his sperm was shaped wrong and couldn't swim correctly. "Some of them have two heads," he said. "Imagine if one of them made it through, and then what would happen?"

That's when Willis showed up. He wandered up next to Clifford and stood there with a big wide grin on his face. His light blue suit was all crumpled and his shirt was undone and there was a big splotch of barbeque sauce on his chest where I suppose he'd fallen over into the plate of food I'd left for him. He didn't seem to mind this though. He was more relaxed, and his limp wasn't so bad. He patted Clifford on the back and then gave him a big bear hug. Clifford reciprocated and then sat down, much to Jolene's relief. Willis stayed up there though, gazing out over the bewildered wedding guests with a wide joyful smile.

In a loud, booming voice, Willis said, "People, I stared into the cold face of death today. I met the Grim Reaper himself, and here I am, alive to tell the tale. Now, I'm not a religious man, for the most part. I think one god is just as good as another, but today . . . today I found Jesus. I just want to tell you all that this wedding must be a blessed union because it has already saved one poor wretch like me. I was out there alone, loaded full of the serpent's venom, when along came these fine people."

SNAKEBITE

With that Willis pointed at us.

"They showed me mercy. They sucked the poison from my veins and delivered me from an eternity in hell! Where's that bride? Where's the groom? I want to thank them personally for bringing on the angels that saved my life!"

Willis yanked Luke and Margaret up front with him and they all engaged in a tipsy three-way hug. Luke's father marched up there and joined them, and then so did the long-haired preacher. Soon there was a whole bunch of people hugging each other in one happy mass. Even Amanda the accordion player and old Mr. Fiske joined in.

Amanda broke away and started playing "Amazing Grace," and Willis pushed them all away so that he could sing along. When he was done, Luke's father hugged him again and they both fell down.

Jolene didn't know what to make of this. "Oh, Margaret," she said, and got up to powder her nose.

Clifford took a long sip from his drink. His eyes were all glassy in a way I'd seen them get before. Most likely he would have no memory of the night's proceedings.

After dinner they cut open the cake and then there was a big bonfire out back and Luke sang a few more songs and everyone slapped Willis on the back, congratulating him on surviving that snake attack. Mr. Fiske pulled out his silver flask again and Clifford took a swig and announced he needed to lie down.

"Help me with him, Georgie," said a voice from behind me. It was Jolene. I helped her walk Clifford over toward the hay bales, where we laid him down in relative privacy. I started to walk back to the bonfire but Jolene just stood there looking at me. I didn't want to meet her eyes, but I could tell there was no way around it.

Jolene let out a sigh. "Clifford can't drive now. He'll be out for hours," she said.

"I'll drive," I said.

"Oh no, you won't," she said.

"I'm sorry about all this, Jolene," I said. "About Willis. Cliff. Luke. Me . . ."

Jolene shook her head. "Such disappointments . . ." she said. I wondered which one of us was the biggest disappointment to her, or if it was just all of us put together.

Jolene's eyes got a little wet and she wiped at their edges. She looked very pretty like that. I'm not sure if I've mentioned how pretty Jolene could be. She was quite a beauty, there was no denying that. It was sort of a shame she'd ended up with old Cliff, actually. At least that's the way I felt about it just then. I wasn't thinking too clearly. I stepped forward and bent down to kiss her. I was going to show her that there were still a few good things left to look forward to. That's what I was thinking. My lips touched hers and she pulled away. It was a terrifically awkward thing to have done. She could have slapped me hard and been justified.

Instead she just said, "Um, Georgie . . ."

"Oh hey, I'm sorry."

"Right, of course."

"Let's go back to the party," I said.

"Yes, let's go. You smell like a brewery. All of you do."

I wiped my mouth with Willis's tie and we wandered back toward the fire.

Clifford woke up at some point and managed to drive Jolene home. They left without me, which was fine. I didn't want to have to sit in that car with them all the way back. I stuck it out until the end with Willis, Luke, Amanda, and that hippie preacher. Margaret had gone to bed long ago. Luke didn't want us to leave and kept making Amanda play songs on her accordion. But finally we just had to go.

Willis and I caught a ride back with the preacher and he

dropped Willis off in front of his vehicle, which was still parked there by the side of the road. Willis said he was going to take a nap inside his car and then continue on in the morning to meet his lady friend for lunch.

"I'm going to ask her to marry me," he announced. "And I want you both to be there for the wedding."

"We'd be honored," said the preacher.

"Goodbye, preacher man. And goodbye, Georgie," said Willis. "Thanks for saving my life. Both of you."

He gave us each a sweaty embrace and then walked away from us. After a few steps he turned around and said, "Georgie, I'd like my tie back now."

I removed it from around my neck and handed it to him. It wasn't in very good shape, but he didn't seem to mind. The sun was beginning to peek up over the mountain and Willis limped back across the road and then collapsed onto the hood of his car.

WENDY, MORT, AND I

was dating a woman named Wendy who was an actress. Or, she was trying to be an actress. I'd seen her in one of those art-house productions where everyone ran around the stage yelling and the plot didn't make any sense. A friend of mine was also in that show and afterward I went to the bar where they all hung out discussing the performance. Wendy had asked me how I liked the show and I told her she was the best part. This was somewhat true because Wendy had been naked throughout the second act and she looked great that way.

Anyway, we'd been dating for about three weeks, close to a month. We'd had sex after our second date. I, of course, had seen her naked once before, so it was a big turn-on for me to have her rolling around next to me now. I had noticed when she was on-stage that she had a large mole just above her hip. It was kind of sexy and I'd thought, *I'd like to be up close to that.* And here I was! It was right in front of me!

We were like rabbits that first month, or at least we behaved how I've come to understand rabbits do, copulating at every opportunity. I've never seen evidence of this rabbit lust myself, but still I suppose the description is apt. It was an exhausting month. I was beginning to develop a theory about dating actresses because I had previously dated another one and she was voracious as well. Come to think of it, both of them, Wendy and this other one, were what you'd call struggling actresses, and so I think my theory, which stated that all actresses have large sexual appetites, actually applied more to the struggling ones. Not that it was a very scientific theory anyway.

Wendy would literally take a running start at me sometimes and we'd both fly onto her bed and land with a flop. Her bed consisted of this big saggy mattress and it wasn't an ideal platform for the things we were trying to do. Her poor neighbors must have hated us. The springs would squeak and every so often we'd roll sloppily onto the floor. I had bruises all over my knees and elbows.

One time Wendy told me her father was coming into town to see her in this new show she was in. She'd been rehearsing it for the past two weeks and as far as I could tell she was onstage for a total of forty-five seconds. She walked on, got hit in the face with a pie, and then said some line about a sinking ship and how it was better to stay aboard than live life as a coward. It was all some kind of avant-garde theater piece, so nothing was supposed to make any sense, at least I think that was the point. I was afraid to dig very deep because her explanation of the "thematic proportions" sort of irritated me. Wendy was very smart and charming and I thought this type of theater underutilized her talents.

Her father's name was Mort and he was a former Heisman Trophy winner. He'd played fullback for USC in the 1970s. He had agreed to marry Wendy's mother, a former cheerleader, only after Wendy was born, and the union didn't last. He tried to remain close to Wendy though, or so it seemed. He would come into the city every time she was in a new production.

We all went out to dinner after the show. Mort had looked me over with a lot of skepticism when we met at the theater. I could tell he'd been through all this before, meeting his beautiful daughter's loser boyfriends and having to pay for their dinner.

Wendy leaned over to Mort after we all sat down and said, "So, Dad, what do you think?"

I was horrified for a moment because I thought she was asking about me, wondering what Mort thought of me, but she meant the play, which, by the way, was atrocious. You couldn't have paid me a thousand dollars to sit through that tripe again. Even the part where Wendy got pelted by the pie was poorly done. Her line about the sinking ship was inaudible because some fellow in a bird suit was chirping on the other end of the stage.

Mort said, "I liked it just fine, honey." I could tell he'd used that response before on many an occasion.

"I know it wasn't a traditional production," said Wendy.

"It sure wasn't," I said.

Mort looked at me with disdain. I guess I wasn't supposed to criticize his daughter's plays. He was an intimidating guy, this Mort. He was still in great shape and could have kicked my ass in less than a minute. I'm sure he wanted to do just that too. Here I was knocking his daughter's acting, about to eat the food he would inevitably pay for, and hoping once again to hump her on that saggy mattress in the apartment he most likely subsidized as well. Boy, was I an asshole in this guy's eyes. I understood that, I really did.

We ordered our food and I tried to keep it simple, nothing too expensive, which would seem like I was trying to take advantage of the situation. Mort mostly talked to Wendy, asking her about her finances and paying as little attention to me as possible. At one point Wendy mentioned that I was a writer.

"For magazines? Newspapers?" asked Mort.

"Sometimes," I replied. "I mostly write fiction though."

I thought Mort was going to lunge across the table and slug me right there at the restaurant. *A fiction writer? Is that even a career? Do they pay people to do that?*

Instead he said, "Oh."

After we had finished eating, Wendy got up and went to the bathroom, leaving me and Mort there to stare at our laps uncomfortably. To my surprise, it was Mort who spoke up first.

"Look," he said, "I don't know what the hell Wendy's doing with this theater stuff. She went to Brown University, for Christ's sake. That's an Ivy League school."

"I know," I said. I meant that I knew Brown was part of the Ivy League, but it came out sounding like I was agreeing with him about the theater thing, which incidentally I did, but it wasn't my place to agree with him on that.

Mort continued on, "I just want her to be able to support herself, that's all. She could do some commercials, some modeling just to pay the bills, and then pursue this artsy stuff on her own time."

"Right, sure, of course."

"Do you know anyone in those fields? Commercials? Modeling? I sure don't."

"Well, not really," I said. While he was talking I had decided that I would do something bold. I would pay for this dinner. This would impress Mort, I thought. I bet none of Wendy's previous boyfriends ever offered to pay for dinner. The check arrived and I grabbed it.

"Let me get this one, Mort," I said.

"What?" He reached for the check in my hands. "Get serious, I'm paying."

"No, really, I'd like to pay for this."

Rather than being impressed, Mort seemed offended by this gesture. Wendy came back from the bathroom and looked at us in our uncomfortable standoff.

"Your boyfriend thinks he should pay for dinner," said Mort.

Wendy said, "Just let Dad pay. He likes to do that."

"No, really," I said, "I'd like to pay for this one." I said "this one" as if there would be many more.

"Don't be a jackass," said Mort. His meaty hand darted across the table and took hold of the leather folder which held the check.

"No!" I said, much too loudly. I wouldn't let go. Mort scowled at me and pulled his hand away. He wanted me dead, I could tell.

I opened up the check and saw that it was for over $150. There was no way I could pay that. I had about $60 cash in my wallet and my credit card wasn't in working order just then. I felt my face turn hot with embarrassment.

"How about I'll just pay for my share?" I said. I handed the check back to Mort with my $60 inside of it.

"That would be fine," said Mort.

"Daddy," said Wendy, "don't make him pay."

"He wants to," said Mort. "I'll let him."

Mort paid the rest of the bill and we went outside. I wanted to go home and leave Wendy and her father alone to catch up among themselves, but Wendy wouldn't have it.

"You're coming back to my place, right?" she said.

"I think I should get going," I said. "I'll leave you two alone."

"Don't go home," said Wendy. She put her arm around me in an awkward, proprietary way.

"I've got to get going," said Mort.

I tried to object, but Wendy kissed him goodbye on the cheek and together we watched his hulking figure stroll away.

Several months down the road things cooled off considerably between Wendy and me. We still saw each other from time to time but that initial spark had fizzled. This was okay by both of us, I believe. Wendy began taking up with some director fellow whom I considered a first-rate douchebag, but I couldn't really complain. He wore an ascot sometimes though, and this really drove me nuts. Who does that?

Anyway, I also found a new gal, a spunky editor's assistant named Priscilla, and we started going out occasionally. Priscilla liked to drink after work so sometimes we'd end up in these strange midtown bars getting sauced until one of us invited the other one home. She was straight out of a librarian fantasy, this Priscilla. She wore glasses and everything, but was really quite sexy when she cut loose. She had no breasts, just little nubs, but she loved to have those nubs played with, even in public. One time I had my hand down her shirt in this midtown cocktail bar when I saw Mort staring at me from across the room. I yanked my hand out and, with nothing better to do, waved it sheepishly to him. He nodded and frowned at us.

"Let's go," I said to Priscilla. "Let's get out of here."

"Okay," she said.

She got up to go to the bathroom first and I gathered my stuff. Suddenly I felt a heavy paw of a hand slap down on my shoulder. I spun around and found Mort glaring at me, bleary-eyed and drunk.

"You little skunk," he said to me.

"We broke up," I said. "Wendy and I broke up. She likes someone else now."

Mort was weaving a little bit. I could smell his liquor breath waft over me.

"You skunk," he said.

"She's going out with a director," I said, hoping that would somehow help.

"He's a prick," said Mort. "That kid's a bigger jackass than you, even."

"You're right," I said. "Wendy deserves better."

"She does," said Mort. He placed his hand on my shoulder again, this time in a slightly friendly way.

"I want you to do me a favor," he said. "Get that prick away from her."

"I can't do that."

"I know," said Mort, shaking his head. "I know."

Priscilla came back from the bathroom and I introduced her to Mort. He held her hand for a long time after he shook it and smiled down at her. I thought he might try to kiss her.

Instead he said, "You take care of this guy." And then he slapped me on the back and stumbled away.

"Who was that?" asked Priscilla.

"He won the Heisman Trophy," I said.

We went back to her place and for some reason I kept drinking. I poured several stiff drinks into myself, which isn't my usual practice, and soon I was too drunk to perform any kind of sexual function. I kept passing out on top of Priscilla and then insisting I could go on. She was unimpressed and asked me to leave.

I stumbled outside and wandered downtown. At first I had no direction, but then I found myself heading toward Wendy's place. It was about twenty-five blocks south and I walked the whole way, weaving around the sidewalk like an ass. Wendy lived in a fourth-floor walk-up and I waited on the stoop until someone came out of the building and opened the front door for me. Then I charged up the stairs and pushed on her apartment door. It was unlocked. Inside I found Wendy in bed with that ascot-wearing director. They were lying there together naked with candles burning around them.

"What the hell are you doing here?" she asked me.

The director stood up with a sheet wrapped around him and got between us. It was a protective gesture, though I could tell he wasn't ready to fight.

I had only a vague plan at this point and the director was messing it up, standing between us like that. I was going to get down on my knees and tell Wendy how great she was and how she could do better than those pretentious plays and even though Mort was kind of gruff I knew he loved her. I really knew that. But that director dipshit was there and in the way. So I stepped forward and poked his skinny chest with my finger.

"You," I said, "don't deserve her."

"Well," he said, letting out a pompous chuckle.

"Where's your ascot, dickface?" I said.

"Get out of here," Wendy said to me. "Please."

"Okay," I said. "But I want you to know I came here at Mort's request."

"What?"

"I did this for Mort."

With that I took a roundhouse swing at the director fellow, but he ducked and I fell to the floor.

To his credit, he didn't kick me or hit me then. He could have done that and been justified. Instead he just said, "I think you should leave now."

Which I did. I turned around and stormed out the door and proceeded to trip headfirst down the stairs so that I cut my forehead on the railing and had to yell back up to them, "It's okay! Don't worry! I'm fine! I'm okay."

My forehead was bleeding, but it wasn't so bad. Sometimes it feels good to cut yourself and bleed a little, so long as it isn't too serious. At least that's the way I felt about it just then. I got to the bottom of the stairs and yelled back up there before I left.

"I did it for Mort!" I yelled to them.

I yelled over and over again. I kept yelling it louder and louder because I was afraid she couldn't hear me.

THE LSD
AND
THE BABY

fell in with an older fellow named Richard who lived with his elderly aunt and manufactured high-grade LSD in her basement. Richard was forty-five and preferred to hang around with people half his age. I was twenty-four and worked as a hotel clerk on the night shift, from 11:00 p.m. until 7:00 in the morning. It was an inexpensive hotel and sometimes couples came in and rented a room for the night but only stayed a few hours. Richard would occasionally bring his dates back there and convince me to allow them into one of the unused rooms without any charge. It was a risky thing for me to do and I told him it made me uncomfortable.

"I'll make it up to you," he said to me. "I've got a plan."

He didn't explain to me what this plan was until one Saturday morning when he showed up at my apartment, waking me up.

"What is it?" I asked him.

"Today is the day," he told me.

"The day for what?"

"My plan has come to fruition."

Richard's plan was that we would drive out to the state forest and sample a batch of LSD he had recently completed. Together we would enjoy the sunny day and expand our minds underneath the big trees.

"I don't know about that," I said.

"What do you mean?"

"I just went to bed a few hours ago. I'm still sleeping."

"You're not sleeping," said Richard. "You're standing up."

"I'm tired," I said.

"We'll get you some coffee. Come on, it's a beautiful day. I told you I had something planned for us. I want to show my appreciation."

He was making me feel guilty for not allowing him to pay back the favors I'd done him. It was a good ploy.

"All right," I said. "Let me get dressed."

"Excellent," said Richard, rubbing his hands together. "I'll be outside."

I put on some clothes and when I walked out to Richard's car I saw that there was a plump young woman named Sabrina sitting in the front passenger seat.

"Hey, Georgie," she said to me.

"Hi, Sabrina," I said.

I'd only met Sabrina a few times before, once at a friend's house where she'd been sleeping on the floor, and another time at a barbeque where she had danced too close to the fire and her long skirt went up in flames. It had taken her a while to notice the fire and several people tackled her to the ground and smothered the burning skirt, averting a more serious incident.

"Is she coming with us?" I asked Richard.

"Sure," said Richard, "if that's all right."

"It's fine," I said, and I got into the backseat of the car.

Sabrina looked back at me and smiled. She was an earthy sort of girl, with long, unkempt hair, large eyes, and a silver ring through her left nostril. Her breasts spilled out the sides of her thin cotton shirt.

Richard stopped at the gas station to get me some coffee and before he handed the cup to me he said, "You want sugar in it?"

"No, thanks," I said.

He dropped a sugar cube in there anyway. As I drank the coffee I watched Richard pop another sugar cube into his mouth and then Sabrina stuck out her tongue and he placed one there also. There was LSD in those cubes.

At the edge of town we pulled up to a low-slung brick house with an overgrown lawn and Sabrina said, "I'll be right back."

She trotted inside the house, leaving me and Richard alone.

"Is this where she lives?" I asked him.

"Her grandmother lives here," said Richard.

He tapped his fingers on the wheel of his car and stared out at the weeds in the lawn. Richard was a good-looking man, for his age. He had a full head of hair and a set of light blue eyes that girls inevitably commented upon. I often thought those eyes were his downfall. They allowed him to succeed in a world most of his peers had long ago abandoned.

There was country music playing on the car radio.

"You want to hear different music?" Richard asked me.

"Yes," I said. "Something better."

Richard changed the station and then Sabrina walked out carrying a half-dressed infant on her hip.

"What's that?" I asked.

"It's her son," said Richard. "She has a son."

"A baby?"

Richard said, "Don't sweat it, Georgie," and Sabrina got into the car.

"His name is Aiden," she told us.

He was wearing only a diaper and a felt hat. His chest was wet with drool. A baby! Sabrina sat him on her lap and we sped away from the town, out toward the state forest.

"Are we dropping that kid off somewhere?" I asked. "Is he coming with us?"

"Yes," said Sabrina.

"Yes, what?"

"He's coming with us," said Richard.

The boy fell asleep on Sabrina's lap, lulled into complacency by the vibrations of the car. Richard had been right about the day. The weather was beautiful. The coffee he'd bought for me tasted like rusty tin, and Sabrina and her child cast an uncertain hue on things, but there was no denying the splendor of the sun and the sky that morning. When we reached the state forest Richard pulled onto a dirt road and drove along until it got too rough to proceed.

"We'll park it here," he said.

As soon as the engine stopped the baby woke up. Sabrina stepped out and nursed him while sitting on a stump. I watched this happen and began to feel Richard's LSD take effect. Things moved by in stuttering frames and my tongue grew larger in my mouth. I wasn't sure if I could be around that kid any longer. He had a somewhat mashed-in face and his eyes were bulbous and glassy, like a frog's.

Richard stretched out his arms and said, "Ah, yessiree."

I thought of a medical question. I asked Sabrina, "Is that baby going to get high from your milk? Is the acid going to get passed through you?"

"No, I doubt it," she said.

"It's pure, no additives," said Richard, as if that explained everything. He took off his shirt and said, "Let's take a walk."

Sabrina hoisted her son onto her hip and joined Richard along the path, one milky breast still hanging out of her shirt. I followed them into the woods.

"These trees are incredible!" shouted Richard. "Look at them! Look!"

Sabrina nodded her head and we walked for nearly a mile before coming to a small creek. There was steam rising from the surface of one of the pools.

"This is it," said Richard. "Hot springs."

He removed all of his clothes and slipped into the water with a relaxed sigh. Sabrina set her son down on a patch of moss and did the same thing. I felt a little awkward then and paced about in a circle, gazing up at the trees.

"Get in, Georgie," said Richard. "It's rejuvenating."

The baby kept making these grunting noises. I said to Sabrina, "I think your baby shit his pants."

Sabrina emerged from the creek like a sea creature, water running in tiny rivers down her belly and over her fuzzy legs.

"Oh, Aiden," she said.

She removed his diaper, rolled it up, and tossed it into the woods. Then she washed him off in the creek and put him back down on the moss. She rejoined Richard in their hot pool and the baby began sticking bits of moss in his mouth.

"Is it okay if he eats that?" I asked.

"Relax," said Richard. "Get in the water."

So finally I got undressed as well and entered the creek. It was only lukewarm, not hot, but it did feel good. Our presence there had stirred up the brown algae that grew on the rocks below, so the water was murky. Richard began to rub Sabrina's shoulders and she shut her eyes, leaning against him.

"I think I'm going to shave my head," she told us.

"Don't do that," said Richard.

I tried to picture Sabrina with a shaved head and couldn't quite do it. She'd look like an alien, or some enlarged version of that curious infant crawling around in the moss. Several minutes passed in uncomfortable silence and then Sabrina said, "I've got to pee."

For a moment I thought she was just telling us this and was

now going to relieve herself in our pool, but then she hopped out and went off to find a spot in the woods. Richard and I watched her dimpled ass bounce away.

"You want me to leave you two alone?" I asked him.

"No. No, of course not," he said to me.

"It's fine, I can go take a walk somewhere."

"Why would you do that?" he said.

"I think she likes you."

"I'm with Carla now," said Richard. "It's out of the question."

Carla was one of the few people in Richard's circle who was close to his own age. She was a wholesome woman who raised goats on a farm outside of town. She refused to let Richard come live with her even though he had tried to do so on several occasions. Likewise he refused to be faithful to her, so they were stuck at an impasse, as it were.

"Why isn't Carla here now?" I asked him.

"She had to tend to those goats," he said. "They run her life."

There was a plunking sound from a pool above us and then a muffled cry. The baby had fallen into the creek. I jumped up and fished him out. He was silent for a moment and then began to scream. I took this as a good sign. He hadn't suffocated. His little felt hat was soaked and useless now, so I pulled it off. I'd never held a baby before and he squirmed around like a wet fish. I grabbed my shirt and dried him off and then wrapped him up inside it.

"Where's Sabrina?" I asked Richard.

"I don't know," he said. He sighed. "I'll go find her."

Richard rose up out of the creek, naked of course, and I noticed then how small and skinny his legs were. They looked like they could barely hold the rest of him up. He shook himself and I was reminded then of a collie, the majestic dogs with great manes of hair who look suddenly diminished once they become wet.

THE LSD AND THE BABY

"I'll be right back," said Richard, and he wandered off naked into the forest.

I stood there by the creek with the baby in my arms and marveled at his weird-shaped head. Whoever it was that Sabrina had mated with to produce this child must have possessed even stranger features than she did. He looked more like an ostrich than a human.

I placed him on the ground and watched as he explored the forest floor with his grabby fingers. I got myself dressed while he examined various sticks and clods of dirt. The curiosity of a child! He ripped up a plant and then stuck some of its red berries into his mouth. This happened before I could think to take action. I tried to dislodge them, but he'd already swallowed some of the berries down. I examined the remaining fruit on the plant and couldn't recognize it as anything edible. The berries were round and shiny, with a clear liquid inside. I pictured a guidebook with their image and next to it a warning: "Poisonous, Do Not Eat."

What had just happened? Was this baby doomed? I listened intently for sounds indicating that Richard and Sabrina were on their way back so that I could transfer this problem to them.

"Richard!" I called out. "Sabrina!"

They couldn't have gone far, but there was no sign of them. I decided to pick up the baby and carry him in the direction I'd seen them going. I called out their names over and over, but Richard and Sabrina either could not or would not respond. I figured they were off having sex somewhere, which annoyed me, but the real issue now was the color of Sabrina's child. His skin had turned a pale green, just a faint tint, but it didn't seem right.

I felt compelled to take action. I went back to the creek and found Richard's pants and fished out his car keys. I looked also for a pen and paper on which to write a note, but there was nothing like that there. I smoothed out a spot of dirt and dug out a message with a stick.

"Went for help," it said.

I dashed back along the forest path with the baby bouncing around in my arms. He remained calm, though he did spit up once or twice. It occurred to me that vomiting would be helpful in this case, so I tried to encourage more of that. He wouldn't do it when coaxed, however.

Every so often I would stop and listen for Richard and Sabrina. I considered waiting for them, but what if the baby died first? I'd be in terrible trouble then.

When I got to the car I placed the baby on the front seat next to me, revved up the engine, and promptly backed the vehicle into a large ditch.

"Fuck," I said.

The car was stuck. One of the wheels just spun in midair. I honked the horn several times in frustration but this was unhelpful.

The baby started to scream then, loud annoying cries I could do nothing to subdue. I stepped out of the car and left him inside so that I could think.

I had no good ideas. I could go back to find Richard and Sabrina, but then they'd just be angry about the car, not to mention the poisoned child. I wished that he wasn't crying now because this meant his heart would beat faster and speed up the processes inside him. I grabbed him out of the car and began walking down the dirt road, out of the state forest. It would be a long walk but I saw no other options.

Shortly into our journey we encountered a large truck rumbling our way. I flagged it down and was happy to discover that Carla, Richard's goat-herder girlfriend, was at the wheel.

"Carla," I said. "I need your help. This baby ate some bad berries."

The child had quieted down now. In fact, he was half asleep. I was worried he might be slipping away.

"He looks fine to me," said Carla. She was wearing overalls and looked tan and healthy. She was an attractive woman, though a little rough at the edges. For instance, at that moment she had some kind of food stuck on her tooth, a piece of some leafy organic vegetable, I imagined.

"He's not fine," I told her.

"Where's Richard?" she asked me. "I heard he came out here with that hippie girl. Does the kid belong to her?"

"Yes," I said, "but we've got to get him some help. Is there a hospital near here?"

"I was the one who showed Richard where those hot springs are in the first place," said Carla. She was pretty fired up. "He wouldn't have even known about them if it weren't for me."

"Listen, Carla," I said, "Richard's off in the woods somewhere. I need your help with this baby."

"Did you eat some of Richard's LSD?" asked Carla. "What's your fucking problem anyway? That kid looks fine. Did Richard ask you to babysit while he went off and screwed that hippie bitch in the woods?"

"No. Look, the baby ate some berries. He's turning green."

Carla paused and looked over the infant.

"He is a little green," she acknowledged.

"Can we go to a hospital?"

Carla peered up the road and saw Richard's car sitting in the ditch.

"Is that Richard's car?"

"I got it stuck."

"Get in," said Carla, shaking her head.

I got inside her big truck and she drove up the hill and plowed into the side of Richard's car, breaking a window and leaving a large unsightly dent in the door.

"That will show him," she said. Then she backed down the road a ways until she could turn her rig around. Then we drove to the hospital.

It was a fairly long drive and the whole time Carla kept muttering about Richard and what an ass he was. I couldn't disagree, but I was more worried about the baby. He was asleep now and every so often I would hold my fingers up to his nose to make sure he was still breathing.

When we arrived at the hospital Carla pulled up to the emergency entrance and said, "Good luck."

"You're not coming inside?"

"No, I'm not," she said.

Just then the baby woke up and vomited all over the inside of Carla's truck.

"Jesus Christ," she said.

"I'm sorry about that," I told her. There were a couple of little red berries lying in the puke at my feet. I was glad to see them. I took them as a sign of purging, and validation.

I made a halfhearted attempt to clean up the mess but Carla said, "Just go."

So I stepped back and let her drive off. She really was a hard woman.

It was evening now and the inside of the hospital was bathed in a cold fluorescent hue. I approached the front desk and the receptionist handed me a clipboard with some paperwork on it.

"I think he ate some bad berries," I said.

"Fill out the forms," she told me.

The baby was awake now and looked markedly better. His

face had regained some color and he was gurgling contentedly. I struggled for several minutes with the forms and realized I didn't even know Sabrina's last name. I wondered if I might get arrested for bringing the child in here like this. He was dirty and naked and someone handed me a sheet in which to wrap him.

The form was ridiculous. It asked for birth dates and Social Security numbers and insurance information, none of which I had. I looked over this strange child and tried to imagine the life he had in store for himself, a life full of ill-conceived trips to forests, clueless strangers, and unfriendly hospitals.

It was nearly time for me to be at work and I considered abandoning the baby there and letting the authorities deal with him. Perhaps that was the best thing to do, wash my hands of this whole situation. I sat him down on the seat next to me and started to walk away.

The baby began to wail and heads turned to look at me. I returned, scooped him up, and jiggled him, but still he wouldn't be quiet. A hefty woman sitting nearby said to me, "That baby's hungry."

It was probably true. He hadn't eaten in quite a while. Neither had I.

"Thank you," I said to the woman, and I walked out of the hospital, still holding the child.

We found a small market where I purchased a banana and some other child-type foods. The baby ate them eagerly as we sat on a bench and I then felt assured that he was no longer in danger of dying.

It was 7:30 p.m., past the hour when I should have been at work, so I got on a bus with the baby and rode down to the hotel. Edna, the clerk on the day shift, was upset with me for being late, but she softened when she saw the child.

"Is he yours?" she asked me.

"No, I'm watching him for a friend," I said.

"Oh."

Edna left us there at the front desk and the baby and I watched old comedy shows on the flickering TV set as the hour grew late. I'd grown to like him, at least. Maybe I had judged his froglike facial features too harshly. Perhaps he'd grow handsome, or intriguingly original, and tell stories of his freewheeling childhood when he got older. Maybe his life wouldn't be so bad. There were so many poor choices he had yet to make.

Sometime around dawn, just as the light was turning from black to gray, Richard and Sabrina burst into the small hotel lobby.

"Where the fuck have you been?" said Richard. He was wearing somebody else's pants and a shirt that was too small. Sabrina, distraught and dirty, had been crying. There were little twigs sticking out of her hair.

"I had to be at work," I said.

Sabrina stepped behind the desk and found her son asleep on the floor, wrapped up in the hospital sheet. She lifted him up and hugged him close.

"Oh, Aiden," she said.

"He's fine," I pointed out. "He ate some berries out in the woods. I thought he'd been poisoned."

"What?" said Richard.

"You just left me there with him," I said.

"He's poisoned?" said Sabrina.

"No, I don't think so. Not anymore."

"You wrecked my car," said Richard.

"No, Carla did that."

"Carla?"

"She came by while you two were out in the woods."

"We weren't even together," said Richard. "I couldn't find her. Not at first."

"That's not what Carla thought."

"What did you tell her?" asked Richard. "Did you tell her we weren't even together?"

"I just wanted to get to the hospital."

"The hospital?" said Sabrina. She began to sob once again.

"Look," said Richard, "the least you can do is give us a room. Look at us."

They did look pathetic, standing there all mud-covered and disheveled. Even Richard's dashing eyes seemed to have grown dim. The sun was rising up now and things outside came into view, the passing cars, the sidewalk, and the trees. Soon it would be another hot day.

"Just give us a room," said Richard. "Please."

It was nearly the end of my shift and I could have found them an empty room where no one would have noticed. I could have written up the slip so the maids would leave them alone until noon. But instead I shook my head.

"You two need to go home," I told them. "Go home, both of you, and go to sleep. I'm not watching after your kid anymore."

Richard stared at me with angry, dull eyes and I swallowed hard.

"I'm serious," I said.

They turned and walked out of the lobby with the baby and I watched them weave away in Richard's banged-up car. I sat down behind the desk and turned off the television set. Now it was finally quiet and I waited for that new day to begin.

BUILD IT UP, KNOCK IT DOWN

I **was on my way to see Alice, my sometime friend.**
Earlier that day I'd remembered that she owed me some
money, so I decided to walk over there and see how she
was doing. I took my dog, Wilfred, with me. Someone else had
given her that name, Wilfred, probably without knowing that
she was a girl. I usually called her Willy.

Before we arrived at Alice's I tied Willy to a signpost and went
into the supermarket, where I bought two six-packs of beer. I'm
not much of a drinker myself, but Alice liked beer. I probably
could have just bought one six-pack but I got two just to be friendly.

Alice lived on the top floor of a shaky house toward the edge
of town. People were always coming and going over there. She
had a twelve-year-old son, Marvin, who was both blind and deaf.
She communicated with him by drawing letters on the palm of
his hand. She was a good mother, but it was hard for her. Sometimes I would watch after Marvin while Alice got away for a few
hours. It was one of my jobs, though not a steady one. Alice paid
me seven dollars an hour, when she could.

I walked up the stairs to Alice's house, knocked on the door,
and then opened it. She wasn't there. Instead a man named Bob
was sitting on the couch smoking a cigarette.

"Alice took Marvin out to pick up his medicine," he said.

Bob could often be found sitting on Alice's couch like that. I offered him one of my beers and he accepted. I went into the kitchen to put the rest of them in the refrigerator and Bob said, "Aren't you going to have one?"

As I said, I'm not much of a drinker, but I opened one for myself anyway, just to please Bob. People don't like to drink alone, I've noticed.

Alice and Marvin didn't return for quite a while. Bob and I sat around discussing his lawsuit. He was suing somebody for running over his foot with a car. According to Bob it had caused him a lot of pain and discomfort. The problem was that he hadn't been holding a job at the time of the accident. If he had been, then he might've claimed lost wages. Instead it was all just pain and suffering, a difficult thing to quantify. A couple of times during our conversation Bob got up from the couch and walked to get something or go to the bathroom. I didn't notice much of a limp. Bob explained to me that when he went into court to discuss the matter he would use crutches and wear a brace on his foot. This would better illustrate his pain. He had a shrewd lawyer and expected to get between ten and fifteen thousand dollars.

Alice walked in holding Marvin's hand. Willy barked and ran up to Marvin. She liked him a lot, more than almost anyone else, besides me, of course. Marvin patted her fur, grabbing clumps of it in his callused hands. He made a little cooing noise and sniffed her back. That was how Marvin identified people, by their smell. Perhaps this was the connection which Willy and Marvin shared, the way they were always sniffing at things.

Alice saw me and said, "Oh, it's you."

Bob got up and gave Alice a kiss on the cheek. I guess they were now dating. Bob said to Alice, "You want a beer? There's some in the fridge."

Alice said, "I sure do," and got one out. Bob didn't mention that it was me who had bought the beer. In fact, the way he said it, it seemed like he was the one who had gone out to get it. This sort of thing bothers me. But I didn't say anything about it right then.

Marvin came over and smelled my hand. He walked with his legs spread wide for balance and his head down, facing the floor. He waved his hands out in front of him to keep from bumping into things.

"Hi, Marvin," I said, though I knew he couldn't hear me.

"He can't hear you," said Bob.

"I know that," I said.

Alice poured a glass of apple juice for Marvin and made him take his pills.

"How're you doing, Alice?" I asked.

"Not bad," she said. With her finger she drew some symbols on Marvin's palm and he got up and went into the bathroom. Sometimes I tried to figure out just what Marvin made of all this. I wondered what he thought of the people and things around him. Did he even know we could see and hear things which he could not?

"I don't have any money for you," said Alice. "Too bad you didn't get here a couple hours ago. I could have paid you then. But then Marvin wouldn't have gotten his medicine."

"That's okay," I said. "I didn't come for the money. I brought you some beer."

"I know," said Alice. She was holding the beer in her hand. I guess it wasn't necessary for me to point that out. Bob chuckled.

"I just came by to say hello," I said.

"Oh, well, I'm glad you did," said Alice. She said it with a flat tone, like she wasn't really so glad that I did, but I could stick around just the same.

Alice didn't owe me much money anyway. I couldn't remember if it was $28 or $35, or maybe it was $42. I had already suspected I would be leaving that place empty-handed anyway.

Bob got up to take another beer from the refrigerator. On his way back to the couch he stepped on Wilfred's tail. She yipped and growled at him.

"Oops," said Bob. He sat back down on the couch.

Willy was still growling at Bob when Marvin ran out of the bathroom toward Alice. Marvin's leg bumped against the coffee table and Bob's beer tipped over onto the floor. Bob jumped up to save it and Willy lunged forward and bit him on the back of his leg.

"Ow!" screamed Bob. "Shit!"

He kicked at Willy, but missed her. I grabbed Willy and pulled her away. I scolded her and slapped her on the head, not very hard though. She wasn't ever a biter, not at all. I guess she didn't much like Bob.

Bob rolled up his pants leg and there were two little red marks where Wilfred's teeth had stuck in. She'd barely broken the skin. Her teeth weren't that sharp.

"I'm sorry about that, Bob," I said.

"Yeah, all right," he said, rubbing his leg.

"She doesn't usually do that," I said.

"I didn't do anything to her," he said.

"You stepped on her tail," said Alice.

"That was before," said Bob.

"She won't do it again," I said.

"She better not," said Bob. He winced a little each time he rubbed his leg, clearly trying to make a big show of it. Such behavior was probably ingrained in his system from all that faking he'd been doing in court.

I got up and opened a new beer for Bob. I opened one for Alice too, even though she wasn't really done with her first one. We sat around for a while and Alice told us about all the red tape she had to go through to get Marvin into the right school for the coming fall. Bob kept rubbing his leg and I felt awkward and decided it was time to go. I said goodbye to Marvin even though he couldn't hear me and took Willy by the collar to guide her out. It was raining then, but we needed to go anyway. We got all wet on the way home.

In the morning I went out to get some food and when I returned there was a policeman standing at my front door. He was writing on a pad of paper.

"Do you live here?" he asked me.

"Yes, I do," I said. For a second I thought about saying no, just out of some vague feeling that deceiving the cops is usually a good idea, but then I decided against it.

"Is that your dog inside?" asked the cop.

Willy was barking at us from behind the closed door. I'm sure it had upset her to have that policeman just standing out there where she could smell and hear him. Once again I considered lying to the police, but I wasn't sure where that would lead me.

"Yes," I said, "that's my dog."

Willy was growling now in between her barks. I told her to be quiet. She stopped growling for about one second and then started up again.

"I'm investigating a complaint," said the policeman.

"Oh man," I said.

That jackass Bob. I should have known he couldn't resist.

"Did the dog bite someone yesterday?" asked the policeman.

"Not really," I said. "She sort of did."

"Either he did or he didn't," said the policeman.

"She's a girl dog," I pointed out. People always assume all dogs are boys.

The cop sighed. "So *she* bit someone," he said. He began writing more words on his pad of paper.

"Are you giving me a ticket?" I asked. "It wasn't her fault. Bob stepped on her tail."

"We're going to quarantine her," said the cop. "Ten days."

"What?" I said.

"For observation."

I couldn't believe it. "Come on," I said.

"Look," said the cop, "it's standard procedure." He certainly was fond of this official jargon. He ripped off the top sheet of paper from his pad and handed it to me.

"You can bring her down to Animal Control yourself or we can send a guy over to pick her up."

"What if I refuse?" I said.

"Then we'll issue a warrant for your arrest," he said, "and your dog will be shot."

"You can't do that," I said.

"Yes, we can," said the cop. I could tell he wasn't really ready to go through with the arrest-and-shoot plan, but I didn't want to test him.

"When do I have to bring her in?" I asked.

Willy was still growling from behind the door. The cop hadn't even seen her. It seemed like he was a little bit afraid of her, like if I'd opened the door he would have drawn his gun.

"You can bring her in tomorrow," said the cop. He walked away and left me there with his citation. That dumbass Bob was going to hear from me about this.

Since I didn't know where Bob lived I went back to Alice's place to see if he was there. I left Willy behind so as to avoid any further trouble. When I arrived the door was unlocked and Marvin was sitting on the floor playing with his wooden blocks. He had this set of blocks which he liked to stack up, one on top of the other, and then knock down. He could play with those things endlessly. I walked up to him and let him smell my hand. He tried to get me to play with the blocks as well but I wasn't interested. I began looking around for a piece of paper on which to write a note to Alice. As I was doing this Alice walked in, with Bob.

Bob said, "What are you doing here?"

"I was looking for you," I said.

"I'm right here," said Bob.

Alice was eyeing me with suspicion because I'd been rummaging around the stuff on her table.

"I was looking for a piece of paper," I said, "to write a note."

"Oh," she said. She went over to the fridge and put a new pack of beer inside it. She offered one to me but I said, "No, thanks."

Bob took one though. So did Alice.

"Why did you report my dog to the police?" I asked Bob.

"She bit me," he said.

"Now they want to take her away," I said, "they want to put her in quarantine."

"So?" said Bob.

"It was your fault," I said. "You stepped on her tail."

"That was before," said Bob. "She bit me later on."

Alice took a big swig of her beer and looked at Bob. "Why did you need to go fill out that report anyway?" she said.

"I had to," said Bob, "for the medical benefits to kick in."

That stupid fuck, Bob. He was always trying to work the system. "Well, I'd like you to take it back," I said. "Go tell them it was a mistake. I'm not putting my dog in jail."

"I can't do that," said Bob. "It's out of my hands."

I got upset then. I don't like it when people get slippery and say things like, "It's out of my hands." I stepped over Marvin and his pile of blocks and pushed Bob against the wall. I was going to take a swing at him but he hit me first with his bottle of beer. He hit me right on the side of the head. At first it didn't hurt but then I felt this sharp pain and my vision went fuzzy.

I woke up on the couch. Alice was wiping my forehead with a wet towel while Bob paced around puffing on a cigarette. For a moment I couldn't remember what had happened and I wondered why I was there. I tried to sit up but Alice held me down.

"Hold on," she said, "you'll get blood everywhere."

I shut my eyes again and I either fell asleep or passed out. When I opened my eyes Alice and Bob were talking in the kitchen. She was calling him a "dumb fuck." Marvin was still fiddling around with his blocks. He seemed a little nervous, perhaps sensing some of the uneasiness floating in the air. I remembered it then, that Bob had hit me with his bottle. My head hurt. I thought about grabbing something heavy and hitting Bob with it, but I didn't have the energy. Instead I got up very quietly and walked out. When the door shut behind me I heard Alice say, "Hey, where are you going?"

I didn't stop. I walked down the stairs. I think Bob said something to Alice, something like, "Just let him go."

There was a cut on the side of my forehead, near my temple. I stopped in front of a store window and looked at my reflection in the glass. It wasn't a bad cut, but it wouldn't stop bleeding. People stared at me as I walked down the street.

When I got home I called out for Willy but she didn't come. I looked everywhere for her but she was gone. Then I looked outside and saw the official notice lying on the mat by my door. It was from Animal Control.

"Oh fuck," I said.

They had come and taken her into quarantine. That policeman knew I'd never take her down there myself. I was feeling crazy now. I was mad at the policeman and that bastard Bob and the lackeys at the dog pound and even Alice and blind and deaf Marvin too. They could all go to hell. I ran outside and got lost about seven times trying to figure out where the Animal Control

Center was. Finally I located it. I had to cross a highway on foot to get there.

The woman at the desk looked at me funny because of the blood on my forehead. Plus I was sweating and out of breath. I looked like a loony, I'm sure.

"I've come to get my dog," I said.

I had meant to say "see my dog" but the word "get" just slipped out. We went over the details of her quarantine, the woman at the desk and I. She was actually very nice. I guess she'd seen this kind of thing before, frantic dog owners. She told me I could go visit Willy, but I wasn't allowed to take her home, not until the ten days were up.

I walked down the rows of cages, past all of those poor barking dogs. It made me even more sad than I already was, seeing those dogs locked up like that. They just wanted good homes, nice owners, and here they were stuck in crummy cages. It was a very depressing place. It smelled bad too, like dog urine.

When I got to Willy's cage it was strange to see her inside there. It looked all wrong, my dog among these outcasts. She wasn't barking like the others. She was lying down in the back, curled up in a ball. I felt sick seeing her like that. I called out her name and she jumped up. She was so glad to see me that she got frantic. She raked her paws against the cage and let out these high-pitched yelps. I thought there would be a lock on her cage, but there wasn't. It was just a latch. So I let myself inside. Willy was so excited that she knocked over her bowls of water and food. The little nuggets were scattered all over the floor and the water made a puddle on the concrete.

I patted her for a little while and tried to calm her down. Her eyes were wild and she wouldn't focus on me. A quick thought occurred to me then, and without really considering it I picked up Willy, took her out of that cage, and began to run with her in my arms. She was very heavy. I hadn't picked her up like that since she was a pup. The other dogs in their cages started barking and yelping. I imagined they were cheering us on. Or maybe they were asking me to take them away as well. The only way out, as I saw it, was to go by that nice woman at the front desk. I was really out of breath from running with heavy Willy in my arms. I couldn't open the door either. So I put her down and yanked it open. Willy dashed through and I followed her.

The woman saw us and said, "Wait, you're not supposed to—"

We didn't hear the rest of it. We just ran, me and Willy, down the street. I figured the woman got out from behind her desk and followed us, but not very far. We took side streets and alleys all the way home. I was afraid the cops would be on the lookout for me and my fugitive dog.

That night I didn't sleep too well. I was worried that someone from Animal Control would come banging on my door. My plan if that happened was to keep quiet and pretend no one was home. I lay there thinking about this and realized I would have to move out of my place. That was okay, I wanted to leave town anyway. I couldn't stay there and be saddled with anxiety over the cops wanting to shoot my dog. I got out of bed at four in the morning and packed my bags. I left a lot of stuff behind, but that was okay too. Sometimes possessions just weigh a person down.

Willy and I left the apartment at about 6:00 a.m. Outside people were just starting to move about. First we went over to Alice's place to say goodbye and see if she had any money for me this time. I'd tell her I was leaving town. That might help.

At first I didn't want to knock on her door since it was so early, but then I heard noises inside. Marvin was awake. I could hear the little grunting and squeaking noises he sometimes made. I knocked on the door and Alice answered. She was awake too, but she looked distressed, like she'd been crying.

"Oh, it's you," she said.

"I'm leaving town," I said. "Me and Willy."

She looked at me, puzzled. "You heard about Bob?" she said.

"No," I said.

Alice walked back to the couch and sat down. "I got mad at him after you left and made him go down to the station and take back that report against your dog. I just didn't think it was right."

Alice's face was white. She seemed really upset and I figured Bob had left her over this dispute. Now I felt even worse. It was nice of Alice to stick up for me though.

"Thanks, Alice," I said.

"Yeah, well, he went down there on his crutches and all, just so they'd know he was still injured from the car accident . . ."

Alice began to cry a little, not a lot, just a tear or two rolling out from the corner of her eye. "On his way back here Bob tried to cross a street ahead of the light. I guess the crutches tripped him up and he fell down, right in front of the traffic. They didn't have time to stop for him. Bob got hit by a truck, some kind of delivery truck, a big one. It killed him."

What a thing to happen, I thought. I wasn't sure if it was actually true. I thought maybe Alice was kidding around, but that wasn't really something Alice would do.

I had to let that information sink in. It was true, Bob was dead. Alice and I had a cup of tea and talked about him a little bit. She really seemed to like him for some reason. I tried to say a few nice things about him, about his funny sense of humor, something like that. Sometimes he could be sort of funny. But the truth was, for the most part, I didn't mind that he had died. He had never been very nice to me. I almost wanted to chuckle because I wondered if his last thought was how much he could sue that truck company for. But then I remembered that his last act was to take back that report against Willy. That was a nice thing of him to do, even if it was Alice who had made him do it.

The morning was passing away. It was getting hot out and still I hadn't left. I decided not to leave town after all. Where would I have gone anyway? I made a plan to go down to the dog pound and explain everything to the woman over there. She'd understand, I felt sure. Our slate might be wiped clean.

Marvin stacked up his blocks on the floor again and I got down on my knees to play with him. Over and over we'd stack a whole mess of blocks into a tower two or three feet high and then Marvin would get this funny grin on his face and swing his arm forward and knock the whole thing over. It was quite an amusing game for him.

Alice drank a bottle of beer while she watched us play. She didn't seem so sad now. "I'll be able to pay you the money tomorrow," she said. "I can write you a check."

"That's okay, Alice," I said. "You don't have to pay me."

"Sure I do," she said.

"No, it's okay."

"I'll write you a check right now," she said. She got up and found her checkbook. "You can't cash it until tomorrow though."

"I don't want it, Alice," I said.

But Alice wrote out the check anyway. "Here you go," she said.

I took the check from her. I put it in my pocket and promised to wait until tomorrow to cash it.

"Or maybe the next day," said Alice, "you better wait an extra day just in case."

"Sure, okay," I said. "That's what I'll do."

Marvin knocked over another one of his castles, laughing as the blocks fell down around him, and Willy and I got up to leave.

RESORT
TIK
TOK

A friend had returned from Thailand and informed me that one could rent a hut on the beach there for $1 per night, meals included. I was struggling to pay the rent on my studio apartment while holding down a shitty job as a hotel desk clerk. I'd work the night shift and when things got slow try to write short stories for publication. A few of my stories had been sold to magazines and though the payment was meager I figured if I moved out to one of those shacks in Thailand I could make things go a lot farther.

The only issue was the airfare. I didn't have it. To solve this problem I enrolled in a medical study where they deprived us of sleep for twenty-four hours at a time and then made us walk quickly on a treadmill while reading aloud from a book. The book was made up of slogans and stupid phrases repeated over and over and many of us got frustrated. If we stopped reading, the treadmill sped up and we had to start from the beginning. Eventually we all tripped or vomited, except for this one fellow named Frank who had incredible stamina. He made it to the end of the book. When we finished with the treadmills we had to drink some bitter orange liquid and then go into a room and masturbate into a cup. It was very difficult, given the fatigue. Only two of us could produce a sample. I was one of those two, and felt proud about it, but the important part was that odd study paid me $1,200, enough to get me to Thailand.

My friend had written out directions to a particularly remote Thai island and I arrived there after several days of rocky travel. While jet-lagged on the streets of Bangkok I'd been approached by a young boy who handed me a pamphlet promising a "Girl with Baboon" show at a nearby bar.

"No cover charge!" he assured me.

Who was I to turn down such an offer? I went over there and sat through several unenthusiastic "Girl with Girl" acts and a "Boy with Girl" act which should have been billed "Fat Man with Tired Person."

Well, I thought, at least there's no cover charge for this.

But then they brought me the check for the two beers I'd consumed and it was $65! Two months' rent!

"I refuse to pay," I told them, but they locked the door and no more acts appeared on the stage. I found myself in an uneasy standoff. The beer was gone and I wasn't even going to get to see the baboon. Or maybe they'd release him to kick my ass. I'd heard baboons were very strong animals capable of ripping humans limb from limb. Or was that chimpanzees? I decided not to chance it. I paid the $65, a serious dent in my finances, and left that bar unsatisfied.

The island was very nice though, once I got there. Ah, yes! It was just as I hoped: beautiful white sand beaches, palm trees, smiling Thai locals, and packs of European hippies wearing little or no clothing all day long. I felt good there. The lodging was not quite as cheap as I'd been led to believe, but I did find a set of huts perched on some rocks away from the beach where I was able to bargain for a reasonable monthly rate. The place was called Resort Tik Tok and I gave them eighty U.S. dollars in advance for a proposed two-month stay.

Most of the beachfront huts were run by cheerful Thai hosts, but Resort Tik Tok was run by a Swiss couple named Rudy and Greta. Rudy was an ornery bear of a man, about forty-five years old, with long, thinning hair and a deep growl of a voice. Despite the idyllic surroundings he seemed always to be in a foul mood. His wife, Greta, was a knockout though, and I began fantasizing about her almost immediately.

Greta was a classic Swiss mountain girl with long brown hair and the body of an Olympic shot-putter. I'm not kidding about this. She could have been on the cover of *Swiss Female Bodybuilder* magazine, if such a publication existed. She must have been fifteen years younger than Rudy, at least. The thing that really got me about her was her insecure, imperfect smile. She had one little fang tooth on the side which stuck out from the rest and you could tell she was self-conscious about it. It looked great though. She could have been a supermodel, at least that's what I thought.

Rudy and Greta had a young daughter, a small tank of a child named Trudi who all day long ran across the sharp rock cliffs of Resort Tik Tok with no shoes or clothing. One time I saw her trip and tumble thirty feet down the rock ledge and land in a bush. Then she got up and ran along on her way. No tears or even a whimper! She was amazing, that Trudi, but it was her mother I was most interested in.

My plan had been to hole up inside my seaside shack and write for hours and hours each day. I'd build up a portfolio and then take the publishing world by storm. I got little writing done during my first month there, however. Knowing I'd likely be without electricity, I had made what I thought was a very clever purchase back in Bangkok: a solid little manual typewriter with stylish metal keys. It sat unused for weeks though, gathering dust on a table inside my hut. All I could muster on that island was a few weak sentences scribbled in pencil in a wrinkled notebook which I later lost in a café. Whatever motivation I'd had to write or generally work for a living had ebbed away. I was reasonably content to pass my days simply lying in the hot sun watching Greta in her bathing suit chasing Trudi around.

Rudy, I feared, had caught on to my admirations, but they had few paying customers and he tolerated my presence with cautious reserve. Rudy had some Chinese characters tattooed on his forearm and one day I asked him what they meant.

"Peace," he told me.

"That's it?" I said. There were four or five different characters there. I thought they must say more than that.

"That's it," said Rudy.

I watched him walk away, this angry hulking Swiss man, and tried to picture the young hippie he might have once been, the man who wooed beautiful Greta, and asked to have "Peace" carved into his arm.

I had been there nearly a month and accomplished nothing. Then an attractive Israeli woman checked into the resort with her French boyfriend and they quickly got in a bickering fight. He left the next morning and she proceeded to smoke hashish and drink rum punch all day long out on the veranda. I joined her in the afternoon and by nightfall we were both naked, pressed together on the single cot in my shack. She was a wet kisser and kept calling me "Jacques," the name of the boyfriend who had just left her. I tried to imagine that she was Greta but it was no use. I awoke the next morning terribly hungover, with the Israeli woman sprawled asleep on the sandy floor below me.

I watched her sleeping there for a little while. She really was quite pretty, and sophisticated too, despite the way we'd spent the previous day. Back home such a woman would have avoided the likes of me, but the rules were different here on this island. Her eyes opened and she looked at me.

"What's your name?" I asked her. If she'd ever told me I'd forgotten it instantly.

"Malka," she said. "My name is Malka. Who are you?"

"We met yesterday," I told her. "My name is George."

She rubbed her eyes and looked around. Her body heaved and she jumped up and made for the doorway, where she puked outside on the rocks. Little Trudi happened to be playing nearby and laughed at this.

Through the thin walls of my hut I heard Greta's gentle voice. "Shhh, Trudi," she said. "It's not nice."

Malka stuck her head back inside my shack and said, "I'll see you later."

I assumed I wouldn't actually be seeing Malka later but in fact I did. She was eating an omelet at one of the small restaurants down on the beach and asked me to sit with her.

"You feel better?" I asked her.

"A little," she said.

We became friends, me and Malka, bonding over the mutual failures that mired us at Resort Tik Tok. Later I confessed to her my longing for Greta.

"That woman is a lesbian," she told me.

"No, she's married to Rudy," I said. "They have a daughter."

Malka gave me a pitying look.

"Why do you think Rudy is so upset all the time?" she said. "He married a lesbian."

I thought about this and could see that Malka had a point. There appeared to be little chemistry between Rudy and Greta. On the one hand this realization made me happy, because it meant that Greta didn't actually love Rudy, but on the other hand it made me sad, because now she wasn't going to end up loving me either.

Malka and I fell into a routine, sleeping together until late in

the afternoon, eating omelets, and then getting drunk throughout the evening. We were both trying to avoid something, me
with my writing, and her with whatever was going on with
Jacques, that Frenchman who'd left her there. I chose not to ask
about it, and in turn she didn't mention the dusty typewriter on
the table.

One afternoon we were lying asleep on my cot and something crashed into the outside of my shack. It was Trudi. She got
up, of course, but then Rudy started yelling at her. He shouted
vile German curse words which I couldn't understand, but made
Trudi cry. I got up and stuck my head out the door just in time to
see Greta come along, scoop Trudi off the ground, and give Rudy
an angry look.

"Shame on you," she said to Rudy. And then she added a few
words in German which made him really blow his top. Rudy's
face turned red and he picked up a wooden bench and hurled it
down the rocks, where it splintered apart and landed in the ocean.
He screamed and spit flew out of his mouth as he rattled off German insults at his wife. Greta appeared unmoved.

That night at the resort restaurant Greta cooked a fish for
Malka and me and we ate it with a bottle of cheap white wine.

"I'm running out of money," I told Malka. "I haven't planned
well. I thought I could stay here and write for months, but I'm
nearly broke already."

"Well, you're not writing anyway," said Malka.

"I know," I said. "I know that, thank you."

When we were through eating Greta came for our plates and
Malka said to her, "That fish was delicious."

"Thank you," said Greta.

Malka put her hand on Greta's and left it there. Greta stared
down at her and smiled.

"You'll join us this evening?" said Malka.

Greta nodded and walked away.

"What just happened?" I asked.

"She will be joining us," said Malka.

"Us? Where?"

"In bed. At your hut."

I couldn't believe it. Malka had never discussed this possibility with me. My heart began to flutter and my throat got tight. Greta! A threesome!

After dinner I hustled back to my shack to get things in order. The little cot would not do. I flipped it over, pushed it against the wall, and spread blankets on the floor. Then I lit some candles and decided to do some push-ups. I was excited. I felt I needed to get my blood flowing properly, perhaps puff up my pectoral muscles so as to appear more attractive. Malka walked in as I was doing this and told me to stop.

"Don't be an idiot," she said.

Greta arrived at the shack around midnight. I was surprised to see that she was carrying Trudi in her arms. The little girl was asleep. Greta laid her down in the corner and looked around at my candles and the overturned cot.

"Okay," she said.

We drank some Thai beer and smoked hashish with tobacco and everyone tried to relax. Finally Malka leaned over and kissed Greta on the lips. Right before it happened Greta gave this little smile, flashing the crooked tooth. She kissed Malka back tentatively and I sat there watching. What was I supposed to do?

Malka removed Greta's shirt and then took off her own. I felt stupid watching them and considered leaving the hut, a coward's move, I knew, but I'd be damned if I was just going to sit there and watch them like a monkey. Then Malka grabbed my leg and pulled me closer. Suddenly we were three people all groping one another, a desperate pile of humanity. I couldn't tell whose hands were doing what. We all got naked and Malka began licking me. I looked over at Greta and she smiled again. I ejaculated on Malka's face. It was terrible timing. I couldn't help it.

Malka wiped herself off and turned her attention back to Greta. They looked amazing, the two of them gliding against each other in the candlelight. Greta began to moan and then Trudi woke up.

"What are you doing, Mother?" she asked.

Greta said, "Shhhh . . ." and Trudi lay back down to sleep.

I joined back in with Malka and Greta but it was hard to find my rhythm. I wanted to be with Greta yet I suspected she wanted to be with Malka, and Malka, I knew, would have preferred her man Jacques over either of us.

Eventually we all fell asleep in a confused heap. In the early morning twilight I felt a hand brushing slowly across my stomach. It was sturdy and different from Malka's. I was scared to open my eyes. I slid my hand over and touched Greta's firm side. Greta! We rolled together slowly and began to kiss. I couldn't believe it. She grabbed hold of me and I ran my hands all over her muscled back and wonderful Swiss breasts. Oh yes! We lay together side by side, trying not to wake the sleeping bodies around us.

I remember telling myself, *You must savor this moment. It will not last or happen again.*

I let out a sound, a groan or a grunt, and woke Trudi up. She stared at us with wide, calm eyes and again I ejaculated at an inopportune moment.

"Your daughter's awake," I told Greta, once I had caught my breath.

Greta wrapped herself in a blanket and picked Trudi up off the floor. They left the shack.

Malka lay asleep against the wall. Perhaps she was just pretending to sleep. I wrapped my arms around her and dozed off.

That next day it was cloudy. It had been sunny and hot for thirty straight days and now it was cloudy and cold. Malka and I walked to get our morning omelets and as we ate she told me it was time for her to go.

"I've waited here long enough," she said.

She went back to pack her bag and I hitched a ride to the post office over the hill. When I got there I found a small bundle of mail waiting for me. Two letters from friends, a book which I'd ordered, a bill, somehow forwarded to me all the way out here, and finally, a check. It was from a magazine. Five hundred dollars. I could live another three months on that, at least. I flipped the check over and over in my hands, making sure it was real.

When I got back to Resort Tik Tok, Malka was gone. She'd left a note on my cot. As I began to read it Rudy burst through the door and socked me very hard in the face. I felt a crushing pain in my skull, blacked out for a second, and woke up with him standing above me, his two huge fists ready for more.

I rolled myself up into a ball and said, "Please stop."

"You took Greta," he said to me.

"I didn't take her," I replied. "I didn't take her anywhere."

"You took Greta," he said again, and kicked at my ribs. This time I did not reply.

Rudy picked up the rickety cot which had been leaning against the wall and threw it down upon me. I let it stay there as a frail shield. Then he took all my clothing and flung it out the door.

I thought of something clever to say at that point, still hiding under the overturned cot. "Hey, what about 'peace'?" I said, pointing to his tattooed arm.

Rudy grabbed my manual typewriter from the table and slammed it against the wall. Then he stomped upon it, crushing several of the keys.

"Fuck you," he said to me, and then he left.

I had this urge to just go to sleep, to just stay there on the floor and sleep for a long while, but my head throbbed and there was blood dripping from my lip. A couple of my teeth felt loose. I got up and examined the typewriter. It looked like a wounded animal, a creature run over by a car. Several of the little letter-stamp hammers were bent out to the sides. Most of the keys still worked though. I could still make words with them. I found a blank piece of paper, rolled it inside the mangled machine, and began to type. I typed out a letter to a friend back home, the person with whom I'd left my belongings for when I returned. In the halted language of that messed-up typewriter, I told my friend I'd be staying in Thailand for a while longer and he didn't need to hold on to my belongings anymore.

"ZEll my Ztuff," I wrote to him, "or don8tE it plEEZE. The RRiting'Z RElly coMMin Elong now . . ."

217-POUND DOG

drifted into New York City and signed a lease on a damp basement apartment in an inconvenient section of Brooklyn. It was a Polish neighborhood made up of three-story brick houses and a waste transfer station which spilled refuse out onto the streets when the wind blew hard. There was a creek too, somewhere, and it was said to be full of oil. That basement apartment had one redeeming feature, a small private backyard, and in the springtime I planted tomatoes there. My landlord, a hirsute woman named Rosie, warned me not to eat them though, because the oil from the creek had permeated the soil. But I ate them anyway, and they tasted fine.

Across the East River loomed the hustle and commerce of Manhattan and I found a job there sorting books and making copies in the library of a large law firm. It was simple, tedious work, but it paid fairly well and I quickly learned how to slip away for long stretches of time undetected by my supervisors. Three nights a week I worked a late shift and remained there until 4:00 a.m. The big firm was nicely quiet then and often I would escape to my favorite back hallway and sit contentedly with a book or magazine.

It was there in that hallway that I first met Jim Tewilliger, the rotund, fidgety lawyer who would come to alter my life. It was nearly 2:00 a.m. and I was sitting on the floor reading when he walked by and glanced in my direction. A minute later he returned and gave me a more careful look. It was unusual to see anyone up there at that hour, especially a lawyer, so I jumped to my feet. Jim was perhaps fifty years old and had lost most of the hair on top of his head. The hair that was left he combed straight back, in thin wisps. He wasn't bad-looking, though his nervous demeanor caused him to sweat a lot, and I suppose this made him unattractive to some. I had seen him around, marching through the hallways in his gray suit, acting harried and important. He was a partner in the firm, with his name printed on the impressive letterhead. This, as I understood it, meant he had a lot of money.

"I'm sorry," Jim said to me. He peered down the hallway as if something there were of interest to him.

I held up my magazine. "I'm taking a break," I said.

"Of course," he said. "Of course you are."

He knitted his plump fingers together and shifted about in his leather shoes. Then he turned around and left. I stood there wondering if I had just lost my job, or at least lost my ability to slack off while at it. I was about to go back to the library and pretend to be busy when Jim returned once again.

"Excuse me," he said. "I'm Jim Tewilliger." And with that he stepped forward and held out his soft, moist hand.

"I'm Georgie," I said, trying to look him in the eye as we shook, a practice I was told businesspeople admired.

"Nice to meet you, George," said Jim. He appeared to relax a little now that we had formally met.

We had a short, pleasant exchange during which he explained that he was a partner and had worked there for eighteen years. I told him I lived in Brooklyn, was new to the firm, and worked in the library.

"Very good," said Jim. "Excellent."

And then he looked around cautiously and said, in a hushed, uneasy voice, "I don't suppose you would know where I might purchase some . . . a small amount of . . . um, marijuana? Just a little bit, of course. For personal use."

I did in fact know where some marijuana might be purchased, but I wasn't sure if I wanted to tell him that.

"I'm sorry," said Jim quickly, sensing my unease. "I shouldn't have asked that. Forgive me."

"It's okay," I said.

"I haven't used the stuff in years," said Jim. "I just think, well, it might help me to relax, to unwind a little. I used to enjoy it when I was in college."

I looked at Jim standing there in his fine-cut wool pants and sweat-stained shirt. He seemed very tired, desperate somehow.

"I'm not a dealer," I told him.

"I know. Of course. I know that. I just . . ."

"I could bring you some in a few days," I said.

"Really?" said Jim. "Fantastic."

"A small amount."

"Right, of course."

It seemed a strange business to be conducting within the confines of that stately law firm, but I decided then that it would be done. I suppose I could easily have said no to Jim that night and he would have said, "Of course," and we would have gone our separate ways. It wasn't that I was looking for favors from him, financially or otherwise. To be honest, I felt sorry for him. Something in his weary eyes and drawn-out face made him hard to refuse. Standing before me in that fluorescent-lit corridor of the twenty-third floor, Jim Tewilliger seemed like a human I could help.

• • •

Three days later I brought three joints to work with me. I placed them in a sturdy, sealed manila envelope and delivered the package to Jim's office myself. His secretary, a wily older woman named Roberta, looked me over and said, "What is this regarding?"

I said, "It's the materials he requested from the library."

Jim came racing out of his office and snatched the envelope. "Thank you," he said to us both, and then he darted back inside.

Roberta said, "Jim's very busy these days."

"Of course."

Later that week I was back up in my hallway when Jim approached. He had a long red scratch running down his cheek, just below his eye.

"My dog," he explained. "She's playful."

"I see."

"How much do I owe you? For the delivery . . ."

"You don't owe me anything," I said. "If you want any more than that though, I'll give you the number of this guy. He delivers within an hour—"

"Oh no. I can't make those calls. I live in Connecticut. I'm all set anyway. I simply want to be sure you get compensated for your time."

"It's no trouble," I said.

"Well, thank you," said Jim. It was nearly 3:00 a.m. and most of the other lawyers had left a long time ago. A few young go-getters, first-year associates, were stuck in their offices poring over documents, and the cleaning crew were moving about quietly with their carts. Certainly all of the other partners were at home in bed, but Jim seemed in no hurry to leave.

"I was wondering if you wanted to take a few tokes with me," he said. "Unwind a little." He gave a quick smile and looked around apprehensively.

"Now?" I said. "Here?"

"What do you say?" asked Jim. "I'd appreciate the company . . ."

We found an empty conference room and opened up all the windows. Jim was giddy with excitement.

"Now, this is crazy!" he said. "Ha!"

We each took a few puffs and then Jim got scared when he heard a cleaning service cart roll down the hall. He flicked the joint out the window and waved his hands frantically, trying to clear the air.

"Let's get out of here!" he said.

We trotted down the staircase to Jim's office, where he shut the door behind us and locked it.

"Ah . . ." he said. He pulled out a bottle of scotch and offered me a glass. I had never tasted scotch and even though Jim informed me that this was an expensive and aged batch, I could barely get it down. I wasn't feeling stoned either. The atmosphere was all wrong. Jim's desk was piled high with stacks of paper, memorandums about stockholder proposals and merger risk analysis.

"I am so wasted," Jim said to me. He plopped down onto one of his chairs and lifted his feet in the air. "Whoowee!"

He sipped his scotch and told me about the various people whose faces smiled out at us from the framed photos propped on the bookshelves.

"That's my wife, Sara," he said, pointing to a picture of a woman holding a hunting rifle. "She loves the outdoors. Very active."

There was another picture of the two of them on skis, standing at the top of a mountain. Jim's outfit was a little too tight. It outlined his protruding belly and showed off his wide, strangely flat ass. But Sara looked snappy in her red snowsuit. They had a son too, a boy named Wendell, who was even more fat, proportionately, than Jim. He was at a boarding school now, his first year. For each picture of Wendell or Sara though, there were about three of a large dog named Boots. Boots was a mixture of New-foundland and Irish wolfhound, two big breeds to begin with, and the result was an enormous, goofy combination of the two.

"She weighs two hundred and seventeen pounds," said Jim.

"She looks like a horse," I said. "Or a pony." I stared at a picture of Boots standing openmouthed next to plump young Wendell, their two heads sitting at approximately the same height.

"She's no horse," said Jim, chuckling. He rubbed affectionately at the red scratch mark on his cheek. "She's one hundred percent dog."

"Wow," I said.

"Sara can't stand her," said Jim. He emptied the last of his scotch into his mouth and swallowed it down.

"She can't stand me either," he said. "We haven't had sex in eight years. Or maybe nine. It's been a while."

"Oh."

"Yup," said Jim. He looked at me forlornly, as if maybe I might have some advice for that sort of thing. I didn't.

"I think I need to get back up to the library, Jim," I said. "Thanks for the scotch."

"Sure. Sure, of course." Jim wiped back the wispy hairs on top of his head. "Listen, this guy of yours, the one who makes the deliveries. Does he, um, deliver anything else?"

"Oh, I don't know about that," I said.

"I'd like to try some cocaine," said Jim. "I feel like I missed out on it when I was younger. Sara doesn't like to experiment."

"You didn't miss anything," I told him.

"But still," said Jim. "I'd like to give it a try."

"I don't know," I said.

"Will you ask him?"

"Okay, Jim," I said. And then I walked out and rode the elevator back up to the library, leaving Jim alone with all those photos of his family and the giant dog.

Over the next week Jim stopped by a few times to check in about the cocaine. I'd thought he might just let it drop, but that wasn't the case. He'd come find me in the hallway after business hours and say something like, "Any word from your man?"

For a while I avoided the subject by saying I hadn't gotten around to it, but then finally I just said, "He doesn't handle that kind of thing."

This was the truth, actually, but I sensed that Jim knew I could do better than that.

"Oh," he said, clearly disappointed. The red scratch on his cheek wasn't improving. In fact, it was getting worse. The eye above it looked a little bloodshot, as if it might be getting infected.

"You should take care of that scratch," I told him.

"Oh sure, I know," said Jim. "Boots keeps licking at it. I made a doctor appointment already."

"Good."

"So listen," said Jim, "if you hear of anything, you know, about the other stuff, will you let me know?"

"Sure, Jim," I said. "I'll let you know."

Although I didn't want to become Jim's "connection," I have to admit I enjoyed finding myself in his confidence. Each afternoon in the firm's cafeteria the employees would eat lunch in tightly segregated groups, the library staff at one table, the paralegals at another, and in the center, at a great round table, sat the partners, unapproachable by the likes of us. Sometimes Jim would be there, sweaty and serious, talking some matter over with another tight-faced colleague. I would stay far away from him then, but I liked knowing that I had access, however shady and tenuous, to that rarefied circle.

One of my neighbors in Brooklyn, a gruff Polish fellow named Wiktor, had borrowed money from me earlier in the summer. It was only $40 and he paid me back shortly afterward. When he paid me though, he also gave me a slip of paper with his phone number on it.

He said, "If you ever want to go skiing, you give me a call, okay?"

I said, "Sure," and thought it was odd that he'd ask me to join him on a ski trip. He didn't seem like the type of guy to be hanging out with Jim and Sara back at the lodge, but later I realized what he meant. Skiing requires snow, and that was a term for cocaine. I kept Wiktor in mind in case Jim ever pressed me about the drug again, which, in time, he did.

Jim came up and found me in the hallway one night just after 3:00 a.m. We hadn't talked in a while and he wasn't looking so good. The scratch under his eye still hadn't gone away. He'd been picking at it or something and it had morphed into a wide red splotch, like a burn mark.

"I thought you were going to see a doctor," I said to him.

"I did," he said. "She gave me some cream. I think I'm allergic to it. Boots won't stop licking at it either. It's a mess, I know."

"What about your wife? Is she concerned about it?"

"She's fed up with me. Everybody is. Listen, how would you like to come down to my office and help me finish off the last of that marijuana?"

I followed him back down to his office. The room was a complete mess. His desk was buried under disorganized stacks of paper and the leather chairs were piled with notebooks and empty sandwich boxes. He had heaps of clothes in there too, some of them covered with long wiry hairs which I assumed came from Boots.

"Isn't someone supposed to clean this place up for you?" I asked.

"Roberta," said Jim, "but I won't let her in."

Jim pulled out the envelope which I'd delivered to him nearly a month ago and he emptied the final joint into his hand. He told me he had smoked the other one back at home and Sara had caught him. She was not pleased.

"I can't seem to do anything right around there," said Jim. "I've moved into a hotel. The Carlyle. It was the only one that would take both me and Boots. It's costing me a fortune."

"When are you going back home?"

"Back home? Never, I hope."

"What about Wendell?"

"He'll be fine. He's at school, remember?"

"Oh yeah, right . . ."

We smoked the joint while sitting on the floor. Jim took off his shoes and appeared to relax a little.

"George," he said, "I want your opinion about something."

He pulled a newspaper out from the mess on his desk. It was a weekly paper, *The Village Voice*. Jim turned to the back pages and laid them out in front of me. There were rows of pictures of scantily clad women, escorts, advertising their services.

"What do you think of these advertisements?" asked Jim. "Are they legitimate?

"Well, sure," I said. "Those businesses exist, if that's what you mean."

"I mean, are these pictures real? Look at this woman . . ."

Jim pointed to a picture of a tan, well-toned blond woman in a bikini. Below the picture was the name Lena. "24 hrs—Adult Bodywork," it said.

"I think the pictures might be fake," I told him.

"How much do you think she charges?"

"I don't know. A hundred dollars. Are you going to call one of these people?"

"I've considered it, George. I'll be honest with you. I have considered it."

"Well, I don't know what to tell you."

"Do you have any experience with this sort of thing?"

"Very little," I told him.

"But you've had some?"

"Hardly any," I replied.

"Come with me," said Jim.

We walked over to a conference room and Jim picked up the phone. He dialed a number and handed the receiver to me.

A sleepy, scratchy woman's voice answered, "Hello?"

"Hello?" I said, looking at Jim.

"Ask her how much she charges," he whispered.

"How much do you charge? For your service," I asked.

"Three hundred for the hour," she said, "plus tips."

I told this information to Jim.

"Ask her if the picture is real."

I handed the phone to Jim. "You ask her," I said.

Jim dropped the receiver and jumped back.

"I can't talk to her," he whispered. "Please, just ask her."

I picked up the phone. "Hello, are you there?"

"Yes," said the woman, sounding a little put out.

"Is this Lena, from the ad?" I asked.

"Yes," she said again.

"The one in the picture?"

"Yes, it is," she said.

"Tell her I'm an executive," whispered Jim. "Very clean-cut."

"He's an executive," I said.

"Call me back when you're through dicking around," said Lena. And then she hung up.

I explained the conversation to Jim and he stood there wide-eyed and amazed. He shuffled back into his office, scooped up the newspaper, and held the picture up to me.

"Is that who you just talked to?" he asked.

"She said it was her."

"Wow," said Jim.

There was a noise out in the hallway as someone walked by and bumped into something.

"Jesus Christ," said Jim. "We need to get out of here." He began flapping his arms up and down to clear the air.

"We're going to get busted!" he said.

He threw on his coat and stepped quickly into his leather shoes.

"Let's go!" he said, stumbling out the door.

My shift at the library was done, but I had to go back up there to get my stuff. "I'll meet you downstairs," I said.

"Don't ditch me," said Jim, rubbing frantically at the red spot on his cheek. "Don't leave me alone like this."

"I won't," I told him.

I retrieved my belongings and then met Jim down in the cavernous lobby of the firm. It was a giant room full of shiny marble and polished brass fixtures. Jim was in the corner talking loudly to the security guard, saying something about the cleaning staff smoking while on the job. When he saw me he stopped talking and motioned for me to join him outside. A black town car with a driver stood waiting at the curb.

"Hop in," said Jim. "I'll give you a ride."

"I live in Brooklyn," I told him.

"Just hop in," said Jim.

He told the driver to take us uptown, to the Carlyle Hotel.

"It's late, Jim," I said. "I'd like to go home."

"I called Lena back," he said. He seemed proud that he had mustered the courage. "She's coming to the Carlyle in forty-five minutes. She said the picture was real."

"Then I should go home."

"No! No. I need you to take Boots out when she arrives. Boots won't know what to do if things get frisky between me and this woman."

"She's not going to look like that picture," I told him.

"She assured me she would," said Jim.

We arrived at the Carlyle shortly after 4:00 a.m. The doorman was asleep in a chair. Jim told him we'd be expecting company and to send her right up when she arrived.

"Certainly, Mr. Tewilliger," said the doorman.

Upon entering the room, Jim was immediately pounced upon by the colossal panting beast known as Boots. She was the biggest, most absurd example of a dog I'd ever seen. She threw her massive paws on Jim's chest and pinned him to the wall, all the while licking his face with her pancake-sized tongue.

"Oh, Bootsy!" said Jim, "How is my little girl?"

This went on for a while until Boots noticed I was there too and turned her attention to me. She let out a deep *woof!* and then lunged at my face with that giant slobbering tongue. Jim grabbed her collar and pulled her back.

"Easy, Boots. He's okay."

Jim's room was actually a suite, and I believed he meant it when he said it was costing him a fortune. The place was appointed with long elegant windows and ornate, impressive furniture. Jim had taken to sleeping on the couch though. Boots had the entire king-sized bed to herself and she'd ripped the plush bedspread to bits.

"Yes, I know, I'm going to have to pay for that," remarked Jim.

He poured us each a glass of scotch and we sat down to await the arrival of Lena. I managed to stomach this glass of scotch better than the one I'd had before and Jim quickly poured me another.

"I can't believe I'm doing this," he said. "I've never done this before. Do you think she'll actually show up?"

"She said she would, right?"

"Right, she said that."

"And you told her you were an executive."

"Well, you told her that."

"How much is she charging you?"

"Five hundred dollars. Is that too much?"

"No, that sounds about right."

"Do you want me to get one for you too?" asked Jim. "I should have thought of that. I could call and see if she has a friend . . ."

"No. No, that's okay, really."

Nearly an hour passed. Daylight began creeping up around the tall buildings, and outside the delivery trucks started their daily rumble down the avenue. Jim was distressed.

"Where is she? Maybe I should go to sleep. Jesus, I'm tired. I waited all night for this and she didn't even come."

He seemed genuinely hurt by this apparent snub. He put his head in his hands and I thought he was going to cry.

"She's probably just running late," I said.

"Of course," said Jim. "But still. Jesus, I'm tired. George, are you sure you don't know where we might locate some cocaine? That would help, right?"

Like I said, I'd kept Wiktor's information on hand for just this sort of situation. I too was exhausted, and operating in a bit of a haze. I picked up the phone, dialed the number, and was surprised to find Wiktor wide awake and alert.

"It's Georgie," I said, "your neighbor. You said to call if I wanted to go skiing . . ."

"Yes, yes!" said Wiktor. "Where are you?"

I told him we were at the Carlyle Hotel in Manhattan and he agreed to come right over.

"I will drive my truck," he told me.

When I hung up Jim was looking at me, vexed. "Now, look here," he said, "what the hell time is this to organize a ski trip?"

I explained to him the hidden meaning and we both had a little chuckle over that. Jim's spirits seemed lifted and he poured himself another glass of scotch. Then the phone rang and it was the doorman saying a "Miss Mendez" was on her way up.

"Oh my God," said Jim. His face turned pale and he began to rub at his cheek.

"Don't do that," I told him.

"I'm not ready," said Jim.

"You've been waiting since four in the morning," I said.

"Oh my God," said Jim again.

There was a knock on the door and Boots, who had been sleeping, jumped up and let out a series of thunderous barks.

"Quiet, Boots!" said Jim.

Boots would not be quiet and a sharp voice from outside the door said, "Put the fucking dog away or I'm calling the police."

Jim held on to Boots while I opened the door. In walked a pear-shaped Hispanic woman who looked nothing like the woman in the advertisement.

"Hello," said Jim meekly, still holding on to Boots.

"There's two of you?" she said. "I'm not working with two people."

"I'm leaving," I said, "with the dog."

"Good," she said. And then she took off her coat.

"Wait," said Jim. "You're not Lena."

"Yes, I am," she said.

"But the picture . . ."

"That's me."

"Are you sure?"

"Yes, I'm sure. What kind of question is that? Am I going to have to get Tyrone up here to sort this out?"

"Tyrone?"

"You want to have a good time or not?"

Lena was practically yelling now and Jim said, "Please, Lena. Would you care for some scotch?"

"Sure. Thank you," she replied.

I picked up Boots's leash and as soon as the big dog saw that, she bounded toward me and jumped up and down with excitement.

"I'll see you later," I said.

And with that I left Jim sitting ashen-faced on the couch, staring helplessly at Lena as she guzzled down the scotch he had just handed her.

It was light outside now, though just barely. Boots was overjoyed to be free from the confines of that fancy hotel room and she pulled me along the sidewalk at a rapid pace. The sight of her giant galloping figure frightened an old lady and caused a group of school-bound children to scatter to the other side of the street. At a Fifth Avenue street corner Boots squatted down and released the most enormous heap of poop I'd ever seen. I would have needed a snow shovel and a garbage bag to scoop it up. I didn't have anything like that with me though, so I sheepishly left it there for the morning commuters to marvel at, and together Boots and I ran across the street to Central Park.

Once there I removed Boots's leash and she dashed about the open fields with glee. It was nice to see her so happy and joyful, even if she was a goofy, slow-witted dog. The other dog owners in the park admired her size and zeal, though I believe they felt sorry for me as well. A dog of that size must be a lot of work, they remarked.

"She's not my dog," I told them. "She belongs to a friend."

When I said that I wondered if I really could count Jim Tewilliger as my friend. We'd spent enough time together to qualify as something like that, and he had certainly confided in me. He'd even asked a few questions about my life during our conversations. But I imagined that Jim saw me as more of an acquaintance, someone who gave him access to a world different from his own. Perhaps he sought me out and confided in me precisely because I was *not* his friend, because I was so far outside his social realm that it didn't matter what I knew or thought about him.

I pictured him now, naked and groping at the flabby body of a stranger in that hotel room. I hoped that it was going okay, that something about his five-hundred-dollar hour with Lena was providing him what he needed.

I should have been keeping a better eye on Boots though, because at some point she ran off into the nearby woods and disappeared. I called out for her and followed directions from a group of startled bird-watchers who saw her galloping down a nearby hill. When I found her she was splashing about the shoreline of a scum-covered pond, surrounded by a flock of angry ducks, and covered with mud. I did my best to clean her off, but the staff back in the lobby of the Carlyle Hotel weren't too glad to see us upon our return.

"A Mr. Wiktor is upstairs," said the doorman, giving me a curious look.

I had forgotten about Wiktor. Boots and I had been gone for quite a while. We hurried upstairs, tracking mud liberally along the carpet in the hall. Back in the room I found Wiktor and Lena pacing about angrily. The drawers of the bureau had been pulled out and Jim's clothing was scattered on the floor.

"Where's Jim?" I asked them.

"Your friend left," said Wiktor, throwing his hands in the air. "He snort, snort . . ." Wiktor made loud sniffing noises through his nose, indicating the use of cocaine. "And then he say he needs to go to bank machine. For money. He's gone now for half an hour."

Lena said, "I didn't get paid yet. He left and didn't even pay me!"

"I'm sure he'll be back," I said.

"Do you have money?" said Wiktor.

I pulled out my wallet. It had $40 in it. Wiktor and Lena agreed to split that if Jim didn't return. It was nice, at least, to see them cooperate like that. In addition, they'd found several dollars in a pair of Jim's pants which was also to be divided evenly.

We waited for close to an hour and Jim never showed up. A hotel maid stuck her head in the room and stared in disbelief at the three of us watching television in that disheveled room. Boots barked at her and she disappeared.

"We will leave now," said Wiktor.

"I'm sorry," I said. "I'll find Jim and get the money to both of you."

Lena shook her head and we gathered up our belongings. Wiktor ripped up a pair of Jim's pants and poured the rest of the expensive scotch on the television set. It fizzled and then something inside popped with a plume of smoke. I filled two bowls with food and water for Boots and she whined as we shut the door behind us.

I found Jim back at work that evening. He'd left several messages for me at the library desk and as soon as I could I went down to his office to see what was going on.

When I showed up Roberta said to me, "Are you the one he's waiting for? He hasn't let me in his office all week. Is he all right?"

"I don't think so," I said.

I walked in the office and it smelled like a locker room. The shades were pulled down and Jim was napping on the couch.

"George!" said Jim, jumping up to greet me. "Where the hell have you been?"

"Boots ran off in the park," I said. "By the time I found her and got back, you were gone."

"I had to get out of there," he said. "I had no other recourse. Lena and I had no chemistry. None whatsoever. She tried to give me a back rub, but I was too tense. Then your Polish friend showed up and things got very uncomfortable."

"They said you left without paying."

"I fully intend to compensate them both. They'll be fully compensated, I assure you."

"You'd better. Wiktor lives on my block . . ."

"I wanted to ask you about that," said Jim. "I need to ask you a favor." He paused and looked at me with a now-familiar look of desperation.

"A favor?"

"I've been . . . I've been asked to vacate my room at the Carlyle. Someone complained about Boots. They said the room is in bad shape too. I'm taking care of the damages, of course. But I need a place for Boots. She's not cut out for hotel living. That place of yours in Brooklyn, you mentioned it had a backyard?"

"It's small," I said. "She wouldn't be happy there. Don't you have some friends back in Connecticut? Or a kennel? What about taking her home?"

"Not an option," said Jim. "None of it. Look, I just need a temporary shelter until this blows over. I'm making some changes, George, and I'd prefer not to have to explain things to my colleagues right now."

"What kind of changes?" I asked him.

"You know, loosening up. I need to break out of this grind. Look at this place!"

"It seems like a pretty good place to me," I said.

"You don't understand," said Jim. "You really don't. Look, will you please take Boots? Just until I get things back in order. I'll pay the expenses, of course."

And so I agreed to take Boots, just for a few days. Jim showed up in a taxicab that night, with the dog and, to my surprise, two large suitcases of his own.

"I'd like to stay here as well, if that's okay," he announced. "I'm not sure I can be away from Boots right now."

I led them down to my little basement apartment and Jim looked around quizzically while Boots bumped into things and knocked books off the shelves with her wagging tail.

"So this is it?" said Jim.

"Right," I said. "This is where I live."

I showed him the backyard and Jim said, "Hmm . . ."

"You might be happier somewhere else," I suggested.

"Oh no," said Jim. "Of course not. Why wouldn't we be happy here?"

We ate a pizza for dinner and later on Wiktor came by to collect his money. Jim apologized and handed Wiktor $200.

"You're lucky I don't break your legs, asshole," said Wiktor.

"I know, I know," said Jim.

"You leave me with your hooker friend. What am I supposed to do?"

"Well, you didn't have to tear up my clothing . . ."

"Yes, I did have to do that."

"It was very rude."

"Rude?" Wiktor stepped forward and slapped Jim on top of his head. It wasn't an especially hard slap. He just smacked him across the top so that his hair flipped forward and left him disoriented. Boots jumped up and barked and Jim said, "Hey!"

"Don't be stupid," said Wiktor, pointing a finger at Jim. "Georgie, your friend is stupid. He is the one who is rude."

"I know," I said. "You're right."

I held on to Boots as Wiktor turned and left.

On his way out Wiktor said, "That dog looks like a horse."

We barely fit into my place, Jim, Boots, and me. Even sitting down we were all on top of one another.

"Do you think I'm rude, George?" asked Jim.

I thought about this for a moment and then said, "Yes, Jim, I'd say you sometimes are."

Jim was glum after I said this. He fell asleep on the couch and was gone before I got up in the morning. His clothes and dog were still there, but he was gone.

That day in the cafeteria, Jim's secretary, Roberta, committed an unusual breach of lunchroom etiquette. She walked up to me at the corner table, where I was eating with the other library staff, and she said, "Can I speak with you for a moment?"

I said sure and got up and we went out to the hallway, inviting stares from the various factions at the firm.

"Jim has not shown up for work today," she said. "His office is a disaster. It *smells* in there. Would you mind telling me what you know about this?"

"Jim's making some changes," I said.

"I see," said Roberta.

"I'm not sure if I should go into it," I said.

"I've known Mr. Tewilliger for almost twenty years," said Roberta. "He's a very steady worker. His wife called today. She hasn't seen him in a week. The other partners are beginning to wonder."

"I can understand that," I said.

"I'm not so sure you're a good influence on him, young man," said Roberta. "This all began with you."

"Me?"

"That's correct."

"I have nothing to do with this," I said. But even as I said it, I knew that in some way, in fact I did.

"If you happen to see Mr. Tewilliger," said Roberta, "please tell him that folks here are concerned."

"I'll tell him," I said. "If I see him."

"Thank you."

Back upstairs, in the clean, quiet din of the firm library, I pondered this conversation and Roberta's damning accusation. I phoned my home number and called out for Jim when the answering machine picked up. Boots was probably listening to me, lying confused amid a heap of my overturned furniture. Feeling uneasy, I looked up Jim's number in Connecticut and called it later that afternoon. A woman answered.

"Is Jim there?" I asked.

"No," she said. "He's not."

"Is this Sara?"

"Who is this?"

"My name is Georgie. I'm a friend of Jim's from work."

"Georgie?"

"Well, we're not really friends . . ."

"Jim hasn't been home for a while," said Sara.

"I know, that's why I called . . ."

I explained to Sara that Jim had been forced to leave his room at the Carlyle because of Boots and now he and Boots were staying with me in Brooklyn. Or Boots was, at least. I wasn't sure about Jim.

"I'm afraid I'm not a very good influence on your husband," I said.

"Really?"

"That's what Roberta said."

"Roberta said that?"

"Yes, and I was wondering if you might be able to help."

"How could I do that?"

I gave her my address and asked if she would come take Boots off my hands, at least.

"I hate that dog," she said.

"Well, Jim seems attached to her."

"I'm aware of that."

We talked a while longer and Sara said, "I'll see what I can do," and hung up the phone. I felt a little better.

That night, when I arrived back at my place, I found things surprisingly in order. The apartment had been cleaned up and Jim was sitting in the kitchen with Lena and a small boy. There was food cooking on the stove and Lena was rubbing ointment on the red patch under Jim's eye. He had taken a shower and was wearing blue jeans.

"George!" said Jim. "You remember Lena? And this is Emanuel, her son."

Emanuel nodded at me. He was feeding bits of bread to Boots, who was happily munching them underneath the table.

"I called Lena to pay her back for the other night," said Jim. "And she came over and helped me clean up. Do you know that you have tomatoes in your backyard?"

"I knew that."

"Boots dug them up."

"Oh."

The food smelled good and we all ate a big meal sitting crowded in my tiny kitchen. Emanuel fell asleep on the floor with his head resting on Boots's furry side and Lena remarked how funny that looked.

"Boots is like a lion," she said.

"That's right, Lena," said Jim. "She is like a lion."

Lena turned to me and said, "My name is not Lena. It's Maribell."

"But I still call her Lena," said Jim. "It's a small joke between us."

There was a knock on the door and Boots jumped up, spilling little Emanuel to the floor in the process. I went out to answer the door and was greeted by a taller, stretched-out version of young Wendell from the photographs in Jim's office. He looked at me nervously and said, "Is, um, Jim Tewilliger here?"

Before I could answer, Boots bounded by me and began licking Wendell on the face. She was very excited to see him.

"Good girl, Boots," said Wendell. They stood there getting reacquainted for a while.

Finally Wendell said, "Is my dad here?"

"Come on inside," I told him, and I led him down the stairs, through my little living room/bedroom, and into the kitchen. There was no one there. The dirty dishes from dinner were stacked neatly in the sink. I opened up the back door to the yard and peered out into the darkness. Jim, Maribell, and Emanuel were gone.

"They're not here," I told Wendell.

"Who's 'they'?" he asked me.

"Well, he's not here."

"But he was."

"Right," I said, "he was just here."

Wendell looked down at the floor and scratched Boots's enormous head. He had grown taller than her now, at least.

"How did you get here?" I asked him.

"I drove," he said. "I came down from school and my mother let me take the car. I only have a learner's permit."

I stuck my head back outside and gazed around the yard some more to see if maybe Jim was out there hiding. But he wasn't. They must have hopped the fence, all three of them.

"I don't know what to tell you," I said.

"That's okay," said Wendell. "I'll take Boots home anyway."

We walked out to the street and I helped him load Boots into the back of his mother's fancy little car. It was one of those low-riding sportsters where the backseat is just an afterthought and Boots looked like a big rug stuffed back there. I told Wendell I'd ask Jim to give him a call right away.

"Sure, thanks," said Wendell, and then he left.

I watched Boots's huge dumb face press against the curved glass of the rear windshield as they drove away.

Jim never did return to my home. He left his two suitcases full of thousand-dollar suits and shiny shoes behind, and months later a man in a van came by to haul the stuff away. He said he was shipping it all down to Mexico. Back at the firm the word was Jim Tewilliger had gone nuts. He'd checked out and left the country. Apparently this sort of thing happened at law firms from time to time. Roberta stayed on and shot me accusatory looks when we crossed paths in the cafeteria.

Several months after Jim's departure I received a worn-out letter, addressed to me at the law firm library. It was from Jim. It said:

Hola Georgie!

    Greetings from San Miguel! Lena was crazy after all. But Emanuel is a nice boy and I took him home to see his father. I have holed up here for now. I miss my dog terribly and am hoping you can help me in this regard. Would you be so kind as to bring Boots down here to stay with me? I will cover all expenses, naturally, and more than compensate you for your time.

    Your Friend,

    Jim T.

I did not take him up on this offer.

ACKNOWLEDGMENTS

Thank you:

Sean MacDonald, Kassie Evashevski, Taylor Sperry, Peter Rock, Creston Lea, Denis Johnson, Kerry Glamsch, Dave Eggers, Eli Horowitz, Jesse Pearson, Rocco Castoro, Hana Tint, Chad Urmston, Adam Ogilvie, Jon Raymond, Lance Cleland, Matt Stone, Trey Parker, Sarah Law.

Taxidermy Writers: Frayn Masters, Kevin Sampsell, Matt Brown, Cheston Knapp, Pauls Toutonghi, Peyton Marshall, Emily Kendall Frey, Erin Ergenbright, and Sarah Bartlett.

Laura Bradford, Emily Bradford, Anna Friedman, Elsie and Theo, Peter and Susan Bradford, Katherine Bradford and Jane O'Wyatt.

Matt Sheehy, who wrote the song "Cold Feet," which inspired the story of the same title, and Courtenay Hameister, who made that happen.

And the MacDowell Colony.

A Note About the Author

Arthur Bradford is an O. Henry Prize–winning writer and Emmy-nominated filmmaker. He is the author of *Dogwalker,* and his writing has appeared in *Esquire, McSweeney's, Vice,* and *Men's Journal.* He lives in Portland, Oregon, and works at a juvenile detention center.